I0672009

RENDEZ VOUS

Gregory John Ferris

Copyright 2021 by Gregory John Ferris
Louisville KY USA
greggjferris@yahoo.com

Copyright 2021 by Gregory John Ferris
All rights reserved
Published by Oak Branch Publishing
ISBN
979-8-218-66148-9

By the same author

This is a work of fiction. Names, characters, places, and incidents are either the product of the author's imagination or are used fictiously.

Any resemblance to actual persons, living or dead, events or locales is entirely coincidental.

Special thanks to Kathie, Lorna, and Arthur.

For J.W. Murnaghan

CHAPTER ONE

For many of the spectators that April day, their most vivid memory was the sight of the girl's long, wavy, red hair.

Pulled back in long ponytail, it glistened and fluttered in the sunlight as she ran towards the elevated horizontal bar, pole extended confidently before her. Hannah suddenly lowered the pole and then planted its tip in the box. Seemingly by divine hand, the high school senior was sprung upwards, narrowly clearing the 10'8" mark, her personal best.

For Hannah herself, the successful vault was inconsequential. It was the moment of weightlessness as she hung suspended that she craved. For a fraction of a second, she was a bird, the goal achieved, its enjoyment too brief.

"Oh, to extend this sensation forever," the thought flashed in her mind.

At the apogee of the vault, in the distance, she noticed passing tractor trailers and cars on the interstate, each sweeping by in their own individual sprints. Her eyes, at the same level as the tallest of the vehicles, made them equals. It was a delicious moment.

As she floated momentarily above the Allegheny Plateau, she saw, beyond the interstate traffic, innumerable trees stretching to the horizon. Even from this height, she glimpsed no further than the wooden walls that constituted her prison.

Not for much longer. She had timed today's jump to coincide as nearly as possible with information from her birth certificate. According to the date and time recorded on it, she had left the ground seconds ago as a 17-year-old girl.

A blink of an eye later, Hannah thudded to Earth as an adult, the sound of her abrupt impact in the pit muffled by applause.

Emily was waiting. "That was great."

Her friend was referring to the vault, but she could have just as easily been speaking of their recently abandoned adolescence. But Hannah's childhood had not been great.

It had been full of hurdles, she told herself for the thousandth time, glancing at the eponymous track equipment that she had avoided as an event, despite her coach's encouragement.

In her chosen sport, falls were unavoidable. If she were going to fall, she preferred that it be from a great height. Anyway, life was a solitary sport, and falls were good practice for it.

Except for Emily, for whom everything was great. She ran sprints, and relay, an event where you could count on others. The two athletes wore the same uniform, but for Hannah the team was a means to her own end. "What does she see in me?" Hannah wondered silently. "Whatever Emily envisions, she is wrong;"

Emily's father was a minister, but she had failed to live up to the expectation that she would turn out bad. Emily's older sister, Mary, she was another story. But Emily, no, Emily was great.

Hannah smiled, and simply said, "Thanks. Yes, it was."

From her position high in the bleachers, Linda watched the competition unfold. Beyond the school grounds, the freeway extended left to right like a wide gray ribbon, highlighted by white and yellow stripes. Further to the south, nestled in a small valley and hidden from her view, lay the home she had been renting for the past month.

"No, it's only been three weeks," she corrected herself. Still, time was rushing by like the trucks on the nearby interstate. It was the same freeway that had delivered her to Brentville earlier that month. It had rapidly become her much needed refuge, surrounded by protective forests.

Less than a month in Brentville and she felt as if she had lived here for years. At other times, it seemed like only yesterday that she had signed a twelve-month lease on what was now her residence.

2

For a year's signed commitment and escrow money to reverse any changes she would make, the owners had been willing to let Linda conduct a few alterations.

Which explained why she was sitting in these school bleachers instead of at home. Home, she liked the sound of that, so much comfort squeezed into a tiny word.

The Venetian plastering in the bathroom was still drying, its strong odor having driven Linda out of doors for the day. The work had taken longer than expected as one of the town's residents was doing a huge renovation of the Vall House, but her bath was finally done.

The plaster was beautiful, the colors cheerful and warm. It was cream and yellow, with splashes of violet and gold, and recalled to her the bright sunlight of a early afternoon in southern Italy, or maybe Malta. The bathroom was larger than she could have hoped for, and it contained both a shower and a separate tub.

She would be spending more than an average amount of time between the gaily decorated walls. It was cheerful, and from its abstract coating she could read imaginary stories, and envision strange creatures, birds mostly.

It was like watching clouds overhead on a perfect summer day, available to her day or night, rain or shine.

"And when the time comes," Linda thought and then pushed the thought away.

She had made other changes. The new carpeting that she had installed on the long staircase, twenty-four steps she had counted the first day, added its own scent of newness to the century plus old house.

Twenty-one days, the time had whizzed by. A bit more than eleven months remaining.

"If you are lucky," another part of her whispered. Where had those precious weeks gone? What had she accomplished in all of her years, let alone in the how many hours that three weeks contained?

Linda faced the track, regarding it without seeing. The races and high jumps, and especially the vaults had recalled

3

memories of her own youth. How much time had swooped by between then and now? Much, much more than a three fourths of a month.

"Enough sad thoughts," Linda said quietly aloud, eliciting a brief glance from a man a few rows down. She smiled briefly at him, embarrassed, and forced her eyes back to the track.

The track could have been hers from her own high school, the same peace and tranquility that lay beneath the tension of the competition itself. It could have been her, Linda reasoned, instead of this most recent vaulter, the girl with the flowing red hair that sparkled under the gold of the sun. Linda was pleased that the girl did not port any tattoos, unlike a few of the previous runners. The sight of small and not so small blue blotches had jolted Linda from her own past to this adopted present. Still, this red headed jumper was more of what she recalled of her own teens.

Linda sighed, inhaled deeply of the rural air and released her mind to ramble again. Brentville had been overlooked by the ravenous future, rendering it irresistible. Pleasant was the word.

"You deserve pleasant," Linda told herself.

A voice asked, "Is your daughter competing?"

It was the same man who had regarded her a moment ago.

"No, I'm just here to support our team."

In another setting, one not so pleasant as this one, Linda would have laughed aloud at his line.

"Your daughter?" Linda repeated to herself. The man was certainly polite, asking about a granddaughter would have been a more logical query.

"No. No daughter. I'm cheering the entire team. And you?" Linda asked.

"The same, cheering on our team."

Linda felt herself blush, and quickly wiped her forehead, removing her broad rimmed straw hat to hide her face and her embarrassment. Was the man mocking her? She felt like a country bumpkin that she was anything but.

"Our team? You've resided in this town for less than thirty days, and you are here only because you did not want to stay indoors and smell the paint dry."

Aloud, she confessed, "I'm new to Brentville but the girls' track team is very good. One can't help but cheer for them."

"Who is the girl with the long, red hair?" asked Linda in attempt to distract this man from her sudden discomfort. When in doubt, let the man talk, had been a long been an effective tool.

"Her name is Hannah Faulor. She is friends with my nieces, one of whom, Emily, ran earlier in a sprint. She is number twelve. My name is Zeke Parks, by the way. Emily's next event is coming up, it's the final event for the meet."

"The four by four hundred relay," Linda asked.

"That's correct. Did you used to compete?"

"I used to participate. In the pole jump, like you niece's friend."

"Hannah," Zeke provided.

They sat there quietly, and then stood as the final race began, cheered as the Raider team won.

"Quite the performance," Linda said as way of compliment.

"Emily runs like a deer," but Linda had never in fact seen a deer run. She hoped that deer did run like Emily.

"Thanks, I'll let her know that she has a new fan."

"It was a pleasure to make your acquaintance," Linda said, as other spectators began to descend the bleacher steps.

Zeke and Linda followed the crowd to the bottom of the stands.

"I'm sure that we will run into each other at the next meet." She turned in the direction of home.

"The parking lot is the other way," Zeke said, pausing for a moment before adding "Ms.?"

"Linda Smith," Linda exhaled into the vacuum of his question.

"The parking lot is over there, Ms. Linda Smith," Zeke explained, pointing.

"Oh? Oh, I didn't drive. I walked from my house on Snowden."

"Snowden? That makes us neighbors, of a sort. I'm a bit east of Shanghai."

"Shanghai?" Linda asked, not familiar with the street.

"Also known as Pickering."

Linda placed in the street in her mind.

"Snowden is quite a ways from here. You are putting in more distance than some of the runners did today. Can I give you a lift?"

Linda considered the offer.

"We can stop for an ice cream or a coffee, if you like, or not," he added, seeing the unmistakable signs of hesitation appear on Linda's face, and which Linda saw reflected immediately on Zeke's.

"That would be fun," Linda replied.

"I don't know about you, but all this exercise brings on an appetite. Of course, my exercise was vicarious." Again he hesitated, then continued.

"The ice cream at Dil's is the best, made with the milk of local cows. They take great pride in it."

"The cows?" Linda asked innocently.

"Yes, the cows included. The cows are passionate. You will discover that passion grows on trees here."

"There are so many trees around. The passion must be unbearable."

Linda blushed again. "Why on Earth are you flirting with him," she asked herself accusingly. "This may be a high school, but you are not a teenager," Linda scolded silently.

"We have some of the best dairy in the state, Linda," Zeke said, Linda noticing that Ms. Smith had been dropped. "Zeke moves quickly as any teen sprinter," Linda mused.

They had walked slowly, and the parking lot was nearly empty. Zeke directed her towards a white Honda van, then stopped at the Chevrolet a few cars from it.

Linda was startled but quickly recovered.

"By any chance are you the mayor of Brentville, Zeke?" Linda asked, adopting the same first name familiarity.

Zeke laughed. "No, but I suppose that I must talk like her. I'm more of an unofficial ambassador, self appointed and immune from recall. The ice cream is truly very good," he repeated, turning toward the school parking lot.

6

"One day I will have to tell you my glass of milk story."

Linda turned and walked beside him. "An hour, and already this man was speaking of one day," Linda thought.

Later, as she lay in bed, Linda reflected on her decision to relocate to Brentville. On the other side of the protective hill, unseen, unheard, and imaginably nonexistent, the world sped by, east to west, and west to east, oblivious to Linda's existence. What joy!

Drivers and passengers remained ignorant of the gem that they passed at more than a mile per minute. Two minutes within the town's invisible confines.

One hundred and twenty seconds and these inhabitants of Linda's previous world were gone, hopefully forever, their passing unnoticed and unmourned.

These strangers still led the sort of life that she no longer craved.

Linda sighed and turned over in bed, weary of thinking of things that no longer mattered. It was a happy state of affairs.

She was overjoyed to be among the bypassed.

The sound of hometown crickets streamed in through the screened window.

Linda did not comprehend the exact words, but she understood their meaning.

CHAPTER TWO

After their track and field activities, Hannah and Emily walked together to Walford park.

"10'8", you could choose that as a tattoo," Emily suggested as they entered the park grounds and walked towards Emily's sister Mary, who was leaning against the front left fender of her car.

"Mary is talking again of getting one," Emily continued.

"What?" Hannah blurted, requiring a moment to understand the meaning of the numbers. Ten feet, eight inches. The height of her vault. It had been a goal she had set for herself eight months ago. It was now attained, now forgotten. The other goal that she had set for herself, would she achieve that one, Hannah wondered.

"Congratulations," Mary said simply as Emily and Hannah reached her. "To the both of you."

"You were there? You could have offered us a ride, instead of making us walk all this way."

"No, sorry, I missed the meet. I had some errands to run. But I know you Hannah as well as my own sister. I was sure that you had won. You both always succeed at whatever you do. You are so talented. Emily, I believe that you could run nonstop to New York.

"And me?" Hannah queried.

"You would have to take the bus. Or"

"Or what?"

"Or you could hop, hop, hop. Hopping all the way, like a kangaroo."

Emily shot a sharp glance at her sister.

"Hop, hop, hop," Mary repeated, bouncing in place and giggling. She was soon joined in the silliness by her companions.

As the trio's laughter faded, Mary spoke again, her voice muffled as she reached through the open window and stretched to retrieve something from the front passenger seat. She lifted one leg as counterweight and balanced on the toes of the other. An image of other girls in the childhood ballet classes that Hannah's mother could not afford sprang unbidden into Hannah's mind.

Retrieving a cake box from the vehicle, Mary continued speaking.

"We didn't come here to discuss world politics, or animals, no matter how cute.

"Unless you want to talk about men."

"We are here for a special occasion. Lets eat cake."

Mary led the way to the park's pavilion, carrying the cake box in the palm of one hand while holding a small pink bag in the other.

Once seated, Mary sliced the cake, passing large pieces to Hannah and Emily, while reserving a small portion for herself.

Emily was pleased to see that the dessert came from the bakery on Main Street and not from outside of town.

They sat quietly enjoying the moment, each aware that such reunions, once daily activities, were becoming more and more rare. Overhead, to their north and south, traffic passed, its sound distant enough to not be annoying, but strangely soothing, like the constant murmur of the ocean, with intermittent gull like honks of car horns. A few men were flyfishing in the nearby stream, and another, further away, was following the hum of the metal detector that extended before him.

Emily broke the silence by asking, on cue, "What's in the bag, Mary?"

"I almost forgot," Mary replied dramatically. She reached into the sack, pulled a small package from it, and passed it to Emily, who in turned passed it to Hannah.

"Happy Birthday, Hannah."

The package was small enough that Hannah realized that she would have to show both surprise and pleasure, regardless of what it actually contained.

Her surprise and pleasure however were genuine when she opened it.

"It's a kangaroo," Emily said as way of explanation, smacking her sister for her previous mischievousness.

It was a small gold coin, set in a gold bezel. On one side was the image of a kangaroo, while the reverse displayed the profile of a woman."

"Twenty-four carat Australian gold," Mary added.

"Wow," was all that Hannah was able to babble.

"I hope that it will remind you of all the hops and jumps that you've done," Emily said excitedly.

"It is wonderful, Emily."

"I found it at Merkle's", Emily responded proudly, as Merkle's was the local jeweler a few doors done from the town bakery.

"You shouldn't have," Hannah protested.

"But she did, and so did I," Mary contributed, passing another package directly to Hannah.

Embarrassed, Hannah opened the second small box, finding a medium length gold chain on which to thread the bezel.

"Wow," she said again.

"You can't trust everything, but you can trust gold," Mary said. "They don't teach you that in Sunday school, or in Monday through Friday school. I learned that in late Saturday night classes."

"These are such wonderful gifts. I'm glad that you were born in the Fall, that gives me time to save".

The subsequent silence was awkward, for they were all aware of Hannah's situation.

"I was telling Hannah about your tattoo."

"Yep, I'm getting a tattoo next week. To go with my belly piercing."

Hannah smiled but said nothing. In her opinion, Mary was volunteering for a black eye to accessorize a swollen lip.

"You don't like it, I can see that," Mary said. Not waiting for a response, she went on.

"My boyfriend will like it. It's a surprise for him, the same for my tattoo. I haven't decided what it will be yet. Do you have any ideas?"

"Nothing."

"No ideas at all, Hannah? That is unlike you."

"That is my advice, get nothing. Why scar yourself for a man?"

In the silence that followed, they heard the sound of flies buzzing around the crumbs of the birthday cake.

"They'll do it to you themselves," Hannah said, finishing her brief sermon to the daughters of a minister.

"Hunter is not like that," Emily protested.

Hannah was confused. Hunter? She remembered now, Hunter was the name of Mary's new boyfriend.

"He's a man, isn't he?"

Hannah took a breath and decided to retreat. It was clear now, Mary believed in the fairy tale. There was no sense in trying to convince her otherwise. Maybe Emily would be lucky. Mary was already a lost cause.

Emily and Hannah would be BFF until marriage and kids and divorce. That was the outcome, wasn't it? As predictable as the start of the opening of trout season.

"If not nothing, Mary, then a small tattoo, in case you grow tired of it."

"Or if Hunter doesn't like it," Emily said, offering unintentional support for Hannah's withdrawal.

"Yes, or if Hunter doesn't like it. I'm sure that you will find something cute. I can come with you if you like, but I might end up suggesting a kangaroo."

There was no laughter.

"How is college?" Hannah asked, switching the subject. Mary had just finished her second year at Slippery Rock.

"It's ok. It's been a real experience. I think that maybe two years of university is enough for someone as intelligent as myself."

"I don't understand why it is that the more intelligent a person is, the longer they have to go to school to get a job," Emily observed.

Hannah said nothing, content to let Mary explain at her own pace.

"I'm not going to study law for four years, when I can make up my own today."

11

"Your own law?" Emily asked.

"Sure. Where have you been living for the past decade? Laws are suggestions. I saw a meme the other day of some generic riot that said, 'Do what you want, laws don't matter anymore.'"

Mary paused to collect her breath.

"Truth is whatever your current professor says it is that semester. Its acting and feeling, without thinking. That is college, acting without thinking."

Hannah remained silent, considering this latest Maryism.

She understood Mary very well. Mary was so transparently inauthentic, even as a child there was something consistently false about her. Dig as she might, she had unearthed no genuine Mary.

If she had believed in such things, Hannah would have considered Mary possessed. But then, if she had believed in such things, Hannah would have considered herself possessed too. She glanced at Emily. "Not possessed," she thought, and smiled.

Mary interpreted Hannah's smile as either encouragement or challenge.

"Our local museum has exhibits on some of the Indian tribes that used to hunt these lands. They had none of our rules. We're headed back to that."

"She talks a good game but that is all that it is, a verbal game," Hannah thought. Hannah had learned repeatedly from Mary's mistakes, while the teacher herself had gained little from her own experience."

"To hunting? We never left. Even Dad hunts."

"To tribes, Emily. Each tribe had its own laws and culture."

"They are going to legalize hunting on Sundays. I wonder what Dad will do?"

"But they are long gone," Emily added, returning to this odd conversation

"Of course, they are. We are building new ones."

"We are?" Emily asked, his voice filled with doubt.

"Its time."

"Time for what? I don't understand what you are talking about Mary."

"Its time to act. The time for thinking is past."

"They taught you that at Slippery Rock?" Hannah asked derisively.

"You could have learned that without stepping foot outside of Brentville."

Hannah stood motionless and regarded this young woman that she had known her entire life. A moment ago, she had announced her big collegiate discovery, that college teaches you to act without thinking. How blind could Mary be? She was the embodiment of just the opposite, she would never act. She would think, and talk, and talk about thinking, and talk about acting. But she would do nothing. She would return to school and follow the typical life path, where acting was left to others. Mary was right, she had found the answer after two years of higher education. Hannah understood that Mary could not, would not accept it as correct. Instead, she would reject it and settle on another less painful truth.

Hell, she could not choose a tattoo without considering the opinion of her boyfriend. There would likely be a series of Tiktok videos and Instagram posts before a final decision was made.

And for that Hannah was grateful to this friend whom she now pitied. Once again, Hannah had absorbed the lesson that was invisible to the teacher. She glanced at the younger sister. Emily at least didn't lie, especially not to herself. Emily was normal, and while that was great for her, normalcy was its own punishment.

Mary spoke.

"You are one to talk. I am surprised that you didn't leave the moment that you turned eighteen."

"I was up in the air about it at the time."

The pun passed, unremarked.

"You can't wait to leave the Brentville metropolis."

"And so did you," Emily added.

"Mary will return to Slippery Rock, Emily. She is trolling us. She enjoys it."

"Its more amusing when you aren't wise to the troll," Mary admitted.

"I'm an adult as of today. That makes me wise."

"Does it?" Emily asked doubtfully.

"Sure, it does. Its magic. As for me, of course, I will go back to school in the Fall. The world has great need of one more attorney, and that responsibility falls to me."

"Me, I am going to stay in Brentville for another year. I'm tired of running ovals at school, and I have no desire to run away from home," Emily chirped in. "I will cheer you both on from the couch."

"Or the diner," Mary said with a hint of sadness, referring to the freeway restaurant where every female in town worked at one point or another, and where both Emily and Hannah were currently employed.

As if reading their shared thoughts, Mary spoke.

"Dad taught us to turn the other cheek, but it's poor advice for an attractive girl in a diner, where the typical patron will grab that one as well."

They laughed together at the truth in the humor. Inwardly, Hannah wondered how many small, hard-earned tips, and slaps on her cheeks had it taken for Emily to purchase the bezeled gold coin.

Later, at home, Hannah stared at the kangaroo. Even a kangaroo could not jump over the trees that confined her. There had to be another means of escape.

CHAPTER THREE

Late the following morning, Linda woke for the third or fourth time. She stretched, and inhaled through her nose, alert to any vestige of the smell of paint. She was pleased to detect not a trace of it. The pungent odor was gone, its flight from the house facilitated by the numerous windows that she had opened the night before.

She had been awakened several times as the sun rose further in the sky, and as the peals of various church bells, near and far, slipped in through the same open windows. Linda had resisted the religious temptations but was unable to refuse the persistent scolding of birds, numerous species who had joined in choir to raise this newcomer from her sleep of the dead.

"Not dead yet my little chickadees," Linda said good-naturedly. It was indeed time to rise.

She descended the staircase, barefoot, clad in old, faded, pink short pajama bottoms, and a new, grey Brentville Raider's T shirt. Once in the kitchen, she brewed herself a cup of tea, and managed to eat half of an overly ripe banana.

"Baby food', she thought, swallowing the mushy fruit.

Linda gazed around her residence on Snowden Avenue.

A year lease signed with the children of the previous owner who was now confined in some assisted living or nursing home waiting to die. This house was simply a more spacious waiting room for the same event. Linda laughed, catching sight of the Catholic church only a few score paces away. Another antechamber.

She thought of Paris and its churches and wondered idly if the steeple of the church next door was the same height of the courthouse, like Sacre Coeur and the Eiffel tower. That could be a chore for today or tomorrow.

After several minutes, she remounted the stairs, completed her toilet, and stood nude in the bedroom. She would remake the bed later, maybe. She considered returning to the inviting, still warm sheets, but no, it was nearing noon.

"Noon, smoon, it makes no difference," she argued internally. Still, she turned away from the bed and approached the far end of the bedchamber.

Linda looked into the small closet that served as her entire fashion collection in this new home of hers. The narrowness of the closet had at first sight appealed to her recently acquired appreciation of minimalism. She had freed herself of stifling wardrobes, of unwrapped bales of dresses, and of the slacks, blouses, and jackets that had once encased her and constituted an important part of her life.

"What a waste that was," Linda thought.

Now, the single rack in the master bedroom closet, paltry as it was, represented a surfeiture of clothing.

"It simplifies my choice," Linda said aloud.

She selected khaki cotton slacks, and while the gray T shirt sleepwear was adequate, it would smell of perspiration that night if she wore in on today's exercise.

"Such big decisions," she thought, then laughed aloud.

A mauve top, long sleeve, also cotton.

"Perfect."

Linda glanced into the tiny closet, verifying that jeans had not returned. She had left windows open, after all.

No jeans were present.

Linda congratulated herself on that act of disposal.

After sixty years in the fashion world, it was time for denim to retire from the scene. She was ecstatic to hasten their departure, beginning with her own trousseau.

"No more jeans! Hurrah."

To complete her ensemble, Linda slipped on her Ecco cross-trainers, relishing the feel of kid glove-like coverings on her feet.

She was ready. Linda stopped and thought for a moment before walking to her front door.

"Are you becoming an eccentric?" she asked herself.

"Yes," came her internal response. "So what?"

16

It was strange. Linda had noticed a certain eccentricity in the first person that she had met in Brentville. She had met him only the once, and only for a few minutes. Yet it had been her most memorable experience in years.

The encounter remained vivid. She had told no one of the conversation but it had been partially responsible for her relocation to this village in the middle of Pennsylvania.

Had that conversation actually happened or was it only the remnant of a dream, like one of those dreams that come late in sleep, just before awakening, delirious meanderings that combined elements of consciousness and unconsciousness into a nocturnal hybrid of truth and fantasy?

Or was it part of an illness? Or was there a third possibility?

Linda hoped that it was truly some local, contagious non-fatal, but inside she was positive that it was something else, the something else that had finally shoved her out of sight of the real world to this...this place."

She was ready. Illness of one sort of another, or not an illness at all, this new, private tradition was one of her guilty pleasures. It was idiosyncratic in the extreme, but each morning, or morningish on Sundays, Linda would walk the short distance down to the bed and breakfast on Main Street, the site of what had been not a rendezvous but an unplanned meeting, from months before, to verify that this magical place had not disappeared overnight like a silly human dream.

When she had stood on the edge of downtown, on her first full day as a Brentville resident, she imagined the painted buildings of downtown as fresh, but, now a few weeks into her sojourn, the cracking dryness was visible to her discerning eyes.

Soon, in a few days perhaps, her eyes would notice other spots where the quaint had peeled, exposing the embarrassed wood below, which try as it might, could not blush hard enough to match the same shade of healthy renovation that was evident throughout most of Brentville.

The town was small, resigned to being archaic in the way that things petite often are. It was content with itself without the tarnish of pretentiousness.

Linda adored it. It was ideal, future warts and all.

She walked half the length of the town's primary street, turned right, descended a small side street, and crossed a bridge over a stream. A white Odyssey swept by her, its passage generated a flood of memories that terminated with her landfall in Brentville and the selling of that unwanted vehicle.

Strange, she had never liked the car. Why on Earth had she ever purchased such a vehicle, one so like a hearse?

Thank goodness that it was white. Despite its appearance, it had delivered her here, to this new and final life. Final for now, she acknowledged silently.

Linda continued past the softball diamond, then stopped to watch another sort of game.

In a level field next to North Fork, a German Shepherd dog watched the man next to him, the animal's tension obvious. The canine's companion bent his arm at the elbow and quickly reextended it, launching the frisbee on its path.

The dog bolted as if released from an invisible lease, ten seconds later, in a mutually designed ballet, the dog and disc reunited. The consummation of the game occurred at a discreet distant, but within sight of the human chaperone. Only spectators in their ignorance and the catapulter in his pride, could envision that they were anything more than means to an end in this early afternoon regimen. The game was played between dog and disk, all else was painted decoration.

Linda turned and continued her tour, directing herself in the direction of the Giant Eagle grocery store.

For years, Linda would shop for groceries biweekly, buying too much, convinced that she would transform the items she deposited in the shopping cart into fantastic feasts each night.

Invariably, after one or two mediocre meals, the fresh items would sit unused and unappreciated in Linda's refrigerator, obstinately unwilling to roast themselves according to the her wishes.

Instead, the ingredients would turn green or liquify, or both, and end up in the trash, and two weeks later Linda would repeat the wasteful process.

At present, the absence of a car discouraged Linda from duplicating her earlier epicurean mistake. It also recalled her time in Arromanches, a small town on the coast of Normandy where she walked everywhere, occasionally taking a bus to other, larger, inland towns. Simplicity was soothing on either side of the Atlantic, but it came with a price. She had paid it.

Linda sighed happily. It was a beautiful morning in her town, and a simple day lay before her.

A white Honda van passed down White Street, a common enough vehicle. Still, it brought a frown to Linda's face.

The girl ringing up her items in the grocery lane had long, wavy, red hair, and as far as Linda could see, no visible tattoos. She was going to ask, when she spotted the name tag: Hannah.

"Are you Hannah Faulor?" remembering the girl's last name in enough time that the question sounded natural.

Hannah glanced at Linda, nodded, and then returned to her work.

"It isn't much, is it?" nodding toward her purchases.

Her basket resembled her closet in its lack of quantity, a few fruits and vegetables and several packets of rice, no eggs or meat.

"I'm not supposed to comment on customers' purchases."

"I won't tell. What do you see?"

"A vegan?"

Linda smiled but said nothing to confirm Hannah's guess.

"I was a vaulter when I was your age."

"Really? At Brentville High?"

"No, I've only just moved to Brentville."

"From where?"

Linda ignored this second question, choosing to respond with a compliment.

"I was impressed with your jump yesterday. My best was not as good as yours."

"We have better equipment," Hannah said diplomatically, and then added, "Did you jump in college?"

Linda repeated herself.

"My best was not nearly as good as yours, so no. I focused on studies and then on work and on other things."

"Men?" Hannah asked simply, expecting no other response.

Linda glanced away, and seeing no other customers requiring the girl's attention, she turned back to face Hannah and continued.

"Yes, on men. Sometimes. And sometimes on boys who convinced me for a while that they were men. Once, a man. Later, men who would prove themselves to be forever boys."

Hannah listened to Linda with such intensity, that only her eyes and ears existed. They functioned solely to see and hear this woman.

"As of now I am trying to unfocus during these, during my time in Brentville."

"How long will that be?"

"You're curious."

"I've been called a nebnose."

"Curious is good. I'm renting a house on Snowden until next April."

"Cool."

"Why cool?"

"It's not. You'll be bored by the first of August. Brentville can be as exciting as watching paint dry."

"I know the feeling. You'll have to tell me more about the town, Hannah. I'm curious as well."

"Yeah, sure. "

"It was nice meeting you. You vault and attend Brentville High, and work here."

"And at the diner, I'm leaving here in a few minutes to work there this afternoon."

"Which diner?"

"Shay's. Everyone just calls it the diner."

"I haven't eaten there yet."

"It's up by the school. We have some vegan dishes."

Surprised at Linda's lack of interest, Hannah shrugged and went on.

"I'm not certain that its vegan, it might just be vegetarian. That is close to vegan."

"Yes, I suppose that it is."

"It's only a two-minute drive."

Linda realized from Hannah's reaction that the girl had no car.

"I'd offer you a ride, Hannah, but I don't have one to offer. Perhaps we will talk again."

As Linda stepped outside, she realized that she had not introduced herself to Hannah.

CHAPTER FOUR

Zeke Parks and his niece Emily were enjoying a light lunch at Shay's when Hannah arrived and went into the back to change into her uniform. Zeke and Emily often had lunch at the diner, in the past it had included Mary, but now with college, and especially now with Mary considering herself such an adult, there were only the two of them at the table.

"You really impressed our newest resident with your performance yesterday."

Emily said nothing, but her eyes were expectant.

"She is renting a house on Snowden, I'm sure that it the Dietz house. Her name is Linda Smith."

The long-term waitress taking care of their table was passing by and asked,

"Is she married?"

Zeke blushed, took a sip of iced tea and replied, "I don't know."

"What's your guess, Uncle Zeke?" Emily asked, happy to pile on. She liked Millie, the waitress with whom she and Hannah had been working for the past ten months or so. She delivered strong coffee to the customers and equally strong advice to the new girls.

"Yes, counselor, what is your guess?"

"I would say no, based on..."

"I know very well what men base things on."

"Don't you have other tables, Millie?"

"Yes, I do. Emily can fill me in later."

Millie had no sooner left them when Hannah stopped by to say hello.

"Uncle Zeke has a girlfriend," Emily said to Hannah.

"She is just someone I met at the track meet yesterday. She is a fan, a former pole vaulter like you, Hannah."

"She is new in town, very mysterious," Emily said, exaggerating the little that she knew.

"What makes her mysterious?" Zeke exclaimed.

"She's new," Emily replied sheepishly.

"She is staying at the Dietz house."

"She bought it?" both girls exclaimed.

"I bet she is rich."

"She might be renting, I'm not sure. Maybe rent to buy."

Hannah's eyebrows raised. She would need to do so research. This woman could float her ambition. One way or another.

"She's a vegan," Hannah said nonchalantly.

"What?" Emily and Zeke barked in chorus.

"I'm pretty sure I met her about an hour ago, at GE," abbreviating Giant Eagle.

"We talked for quite a while. Its too bad she doesn't have a car. She seems a bit odd," Hannah remarked about Linda.

"She will fit in well," Emily laughed delightedly.

Zeke stared at Hannah, amazed at her knowledge about this woman that he had himself only so recently encountered.

"Is her name Linda Smith?" Zeke queried and smiled in triumph when Hannah admitted that the woman had not introduced herself by name.

"Is ice cream vegan?" Zeke asked.

"I think so," Hannah replied, while Emily simply shrugged.

Zeke noticed the men at a neighboring table, a group of anglers.

"Are they yours?" he asked Hannah.

"Yes, I'd better go."

"They never order fish," Zeke commented as Hannah turned and left.

Hannah was not thinking of fish, nor of ice cream. She would soon be on a first name basis with the new woman, calling her Mrs. Boomer or whatever her name was, oh yes, Ms. Smith. A new woman in town. That itself was a rarity. The woman intrigued her. One day, Hannah herself would be the new woman of mystery in a town far from Brentville. Hannah's eyebrows raised. Yes, she would need to do some research

The anglers were gray haired with the exception of one young man, likely the grandson of one of the other men. He caught Hannah's eye.

She recognized that he was bad, which usually meant a good tip, if he had any money, which he didn't. Otherwise, he would not be here with gramps and gramp's' friends. Still, he might be useful at prying a tip from them. Men never learn. Not even Zeke.

The boy regarded Hannah while pretending to listen to his grandfather and his grandfather's friend discuss fishing. The boy was a man in his own eyes, his facial hair was as valuable to him as a tattoo would be to Mary Parks.

This redheaded waitress wasn't a farm girl exactly, but neither was she like the few women from Pittsburgh that he had experience with.

The oblong object carried prominently in a rear jeans pocket was the only similarity, but that was the universal fashion. The flat rectangular outline of her phone drew attention to her curves. The hardness and clarity of its screen was as compelling to her sex as she was to him.

This girl was soft where the others were hard, and hard where the others were brittle.

He couldn't describe the woman of his dreams, but in this roadside restaurant he had stumbled across the nearest facsimile. She met his ambiguous criteria, she punched all the buttons, and she pressed his.

She was the perfect target of his burgeoning desire Her body language spoke of yearning for violent offense. He could assist her with that need.

CHAPTER FIVE

Hannah stared out the classroom window and frowned. In the distance, life sped by on the freeway, while she sat here and studied the actions and words of the long since dead. If she tired of that, she could walk a few hundred yards from the schoolgrounds and speak to them directly in the cemetery. From teen to enterred was just a skip away.

"A few more weeks of modern school, where modern kids are anti socialized and deeducated," Hannah thought.

The school and the graveyard were separated by a small ball field, where the business of her life, the fun part, was confined.

Vehicles whizzed by on the freeway, her world a blur to them. Seated in a classroom seat, Hannah felt that she was approaching the short upright, gray markers to the east as rapidly as the Amazon tractor trailer had just done.

Emily entered the nearly empty room; she too was frowning.

"Is Mary off to be branded?"

"If she is, she hasn't notified me."

"Hunter won't like, no matter what design she picks."

"She talks about it as if it is solely her concern, her tattoo, her belly"

"Stabbing," interjected Hannah

"Piercing," continued Emily.

"Whatever."

"Its all about her."

"Or so she screams."

Emily frowned at the second insult.

Hannah ignored her friend's disapproval.

"But then she acts like a woman from an old black and white TV show."

"Do you watch those?"

"No. But Mary must. She is all talk, you know that, Emily. She is your sister."

"I'm tired of talking about her. She will do what she wants"

"And so will I."

"Me too, Hannah."

'I'm not going to prom, last year's was a waste of time."

"Peter told me this morning that he isn't going to ask me."

"But he already did."

"He took it back."

"Jerk."

"He is no Hunter."

"What reason did he give to you?" Hannah suspected another girl but was hesitant to suggest it.

"He is using the money for his car; he'll need it for college."

"Peter doesn't plan very well."

"On the contrary, Peter is very methodical. I just realized what he had known for weeks, or longer. His plans don't include me. Why is everyone so anxious to leave Brentville?"

Hannah had no answer that she hadn't confided to Emily a hundred times.

"I consider this my last high school lesson."

Hannah remained silent, anticipating more.

Instead, Emily said flatly,

"At least I won't have to return a dress."

Promises are supposed to be for the young. The old have exhausted all of theirs. Hannah felt bad for Emily.

"I'm sorry to hear that, Emily. About the dress, I mean."

"You're not, but thanks for saying that you are. No one is sorry, not you, not Peter, and not me."

CHAPTER SIX

It was a Wednesday, the only structured day of Linda's week. It was the day that she dreaded, the day that she forced herself to rejoin temporarily the world as it was. She felt an Amish, mingling with the English.

But work could wait until after her visit to the YMCA, an unexpected diamond in this golden town. It was said by many to be the smallest full-service YMCA east of the Mississippi. It was said by Linda to be perfect.

Linda could immerse herself in the water, alongside others who enjoyed the same basic pleasure of temporary weightlessness.

The woman was blondish and thinnish, the man ported short hair. Sunlight streamed in from windows set high in the south facing wall. Reflections from their wedding bands bounced across the same wall and ceiling like poorly directed tennis balls. The sun's rays found no visible tattoos to illuminate, so they settled on the couple's two children.

Linda despised what people did to themselves in these so-called modern times. It's terrible scar tissue or tattoos, both mark you literally or figuratively as part of this or that cult. Even the untouched consider themselves marked.

Linda had hoped that the town would be full of such undamaged families, a town that would strike some as bizarre due to its simplicity and ordinariness.

The daughter of this unremarkable family, about five years of age, Linda estimated, wore a mermaid swimsuit, complete with an aqua-marine tail.

"Reality goes much better with a dose of fantasy," Linda smiled.

Following her swim, Linda strolled the block and a half to the café for a light breakfast and a cup of tea. Seated alone at a table, she looked up to see a stranger outside the café, peering in. He opened the door and stepped partway in, hesitating on the threshold. He scanned the dining room and then the counter, where stools sat empty, interspersed with columns that stretched to the tin ceiling

Linda waved, but if he saw her invitation to join her, he ignored it. His head continued to scan the small facility, and then he turned and left, closing the wooden framed glass door behind him.

"He was counting," the waitress, Virginia, explained.

"Counting what?"

"People".

Linda nodded, then asked, "Is he a health inspector?"

Virginia laughed.

"No, not hardly. That is Mike Hayes. Unless we're over a certain number, he won't enter."

Linda looked around, but before she could begin, the server finished Linda's task.

"Seven," she said.

Linda's gaze snapped back to the server.

"There are seven people in here. Visible, that is. His magic number is eight or nine, as near as I can determine."

Linda looked confused.

"Unless there are eight or nine, or more people, Mike won't enter a restaurant or a business, or a home."

"That's odd."

"Do you think?" Virginia agreed.

"We were so close," she continued. "Sometimes he waits, sometimes he leaves."

"Why does he count?"

"Who knows? Why does anyone do anything? That's why I like working here, because people have to eat to live."

"I guess that provides an answer to your question."

"Indeed, it does. I know why folks are here. I don't worry about any of the other questions. Of course, Mike's magic people number doesn't apply to churches."

"Hmm," Linda hummed as way of encouragement.

28

"Yep, churches are an exception. God must count for a lot. That didn't come out the way it sounded," she added hurriedly.

"I understand," offered Linda.

"But homes, and business, nope, they have minimums, quotas you might call it."

"I see, I guess," Linda said.

"The strange part is that Mike lives alone, in a small apartment on Cole. But its still a free country, isn't it? So, what would you like today, other than coffee? You gotta eat, just like the rest of us."

Linda was distracted. She stirred the cream into the coffee in the cup that was set before her, and then stared at, surprised at its light color. Did I do that, she asked, puzzled, and then giggled, embarrassed at this self-disclosure.

She opened the copy of the Wall Street Journal that she had brought into the cafe, regarding the paper's front page without focusing on any of the words.

"Is there any advice in there on keeping the world at bay?"

Linda gazed upward, her eyes coming to rest on the face of Zeke Parks. She smiled.

"I'm waiting," Zeke persisted good naturedly.

"I had convinced myself that you were our newest hermit, a female version of our Mike Hayes. What happened to your wall of exile?", pointing to the paper.

"Its what remains of lifeline to the world. I have it only because I need it."

Zeke nodded noncommittally.

"I read it when it is about a week old, see?" Linda continued, showing him the front page, her left index finger touching the date. He could read the date, it was from last Thursday, but he reached over to move her hand a bit to his left.

"So it is," he said, his voice dry.

"Do you mind?" he said, reaching for her untouched glass of water and taking a small sip from it.

"And I read one of these per week. After a week, the news has mellowed, and if the world has come to an end, I haven't had to read about it."

She paused, then switched the subject.

"You look distracted. Is everything ok?"

Zeke wasn't sure.

"It seems better than ok," he answered cryptically.

Today's breakfast was not going as either of them was accustomed.

"Do you pay for the paper?" That's a stupid question, he thought, as did Linda. But it served to return the drift of the conversation to more normal if shallower waters.

"Yes," Linda answered.

"For an entire week? "

"Yes."

"For one seven-day old newspaper?"

"Full price. Gary at Fieman's holds the Thursday edition for me. I wonder if he reads it beforehand, or if he is somehow living in a 6/7s world that is partially obscured."

"That would be better than most of us."

"If I want more of the world's lies, I can open my electronic. But I use that only for..." The message trailed off.

"I think that the news is like an apple. In small does the arsenic in the seeds won't kill you."

"You might be right about that."

"Gary hangs the newspaper behind the counter like a small side of beef. Most of the untruths in it have broken down, and I find them more palatable."

"What was the crisis last week, I seem to have forgotten."

"Mexican Cultural Appropriation."

"More cultural appropriation. Isn't it about time they abbreviate that phrase? It's quite a mouthful."

"Its all so silly. Six hundred years ago Mexican culture had no Spanish, no Christianity. No bullfights either."

"What about pina coladas?"

"Nope."

"That one is a pity."

"Yes, it is."

"Columbus brought different cultures to half the planet, all in three tiny ships. Why he isn't the patron saint of diversity is beyond me."

Zeke nodded.

"What is the big lie today?"

"I haven't had time to find it, I'm sure its as ridiculous as the previous ones."

"As for me Linda, I if wanted to pay for old lies, I'd still be making the bar rounds."

"Oh?"

"I've heard tall tales from every single or divorced woman in Armstrong County who has taken a barstool next to me."

"That sounds like a tall tale of a man from Jefferson County."

"Look at this story for example," he said, stabbing the head of a different article, "'Cannibals cooking up a comeback?'"

"I don't read articles or books that end in a question mark.

I have enough questions in my life, why waste time on those of strangers who can't or won't take a stance."

"That's good advice. Still, I wonder if he would be convicted here, where there are probably more cannibals than vegans and pot smokers combined."

"Really?"

"I have no idea. People invent such weird stories."

"Including your Armstrong amours?"

"Women, not amours."

Linda and Zeke walked back together for a minute from the café, before separating in front of the courthouse to go their own way.

She passed the civil defense sign that indicated the way to whatever remained of the 1950s underground bomb shelter. It was still available in case of stupidity, proof that the reason and rationality demonstrated in court above was lacking in the world at large.

The mailman had made his daily delivery, and the weekly Wednesday package from FedEx stood propped against the front door, trying to force its way in.

Linda could no longer delay this painful duty.

She went through the mail as rapidly as possible, discarding almost all of it into the shredder. The FedEx package with her financial accounts she went through more carefully, for they were what would keep her going until... And the gold, the gold she had required no weekly review, no vigilance from computer error. It was content to bask in itself. Still, she needed to do something with it. Soon.

As for the paperwork, maybe she should burn it instead of consigning it to some rural landfill. Another chore.

And a few moments with the electronic devil, a punishment now.

Even monks offered homage only five times per day. She no longer checked the weather in distant cities, nor followed one link to another like a faithful bloodhound. Uninteresting news written about uninteresting celebrities nolonger interested her.

And now, a few weeks later, she rarely felt the craving for screen. This was a necessity, like cleaning the toilet bowl weekly. Her days were longer, as well her nights, no longer delayed by a small rectangle of pale light. She was freer, if not free.

She found herself looking at the world, her head level, not bowed to Apple.

CHAPTER SEVEN

Hannah stood at the side of North Fork where it flowed underneath the spans of the interstate.

She was tempted to throw stones into the stream, but that served no purpose.

It would only irritate the fish, who would not complain, as well as the nearby anglers, who would.

Between the east and westbound lanes, she could look up, and dream of choosing between them, beginning her life's journey simply by selecting one direction over another.

She watched the anglers. They must think themselves clever, tricking fish. Ultimately it was the fish that made the decision, just like women she thought suddenly. How dumb men were. She laughed aloud, a few of the nearer men heard the sound over the rushing water in which they stood and cast a glance in her direction. She ignored their lures.

She was not a fish, but what was she? A hunter, she decided.

Men were sugar daddies, fattening.

One man had enthused that he wanted to grow old with her. She was too polite to point out to him that he was already there.

She looked again at the anglers. They had money, their expensive gear and sixty-thousand-dollar SUVs testified to their wealth. A few likely had a case of widower, and all were slowly overdosing on age.

No, she was not willing to attend to a sugar daddy, and absolutely not a sugar granddaddy.

Still, their cars were nice, she couldn't afford to cross all of these wallets off her list.

Men were not an end; she had enough experience with the local variety along with the transient forms that floated by like invasive seaweed attempting to snare her. She was not complaisant to stop and let one drown her.

Men were not an end, although she wasn't sure what constituted an appropriate ending. She was just beginning. She could worry about ending and meaning later. As far as she knew, there might be no ending whatsoever.

Men were not an end but could serve her start. Perhaps she would discover one worth more than throwing back, she told herself, watching one of the aged anglers release a trout into the cold of North Fork.

The guests at the diner where she worked, and at the B&B, where she used to work, were nothing special, and yet the way they bragged self deprecatingly of their to them drab lives was incredibly glamorous compared to her own. Her mouth grew tight at the thought of an equally bleak future.

Hannah remembered the boy with the anglers in the café. Maybe she would run into him again, he was certainly interested in her, and she might find his interest useful. Her face relaxed.

"But that couple," she thought of her most recent customers, "what a waste." Her lips pulled into a straight line, taut with disgust.

Hannah had been amazed that either of the pair was able to eat a bite, they were both so full of crap. They were poorly educated, to the point of total incomprehension. "Make a decision and move on," she wanted to shout. They had hesitated over the menu, as if it had been written in a foreign language, with each item new and exotic. "They must be six-year-olds in adult bodies," she had thought at the time, and her fear that they had no concept of tipping had been warranted.

Overhead, the flow of traffic continued unabated.
If the wind was blowing strong, it carried with it the mocking sound of tires as they traversed the expansion joint, a cry as familiar to her as the taunting screeches of blue jays.

Each vehicle carried travelers to their wonderful future. They were futures denied her, sitting next to the Brentville water plant.

"Hello Hannah".

Hannah looked up to see the woman that she had spoken with at GE.

"Remember me, we met the other day?"

"Oh sure. You are Linda Smith."

Linda's eyebrows raised in surprise.

"Zeke Parks told us about you. At the diner."

"This is a small town," Linda said good-naturedly.

Hannah's mind began to race, all thought of the boy from the café erased.

"I'm not interrupting you, am I?"

"I come here to think. Its my own magic place."

"Well in that case..."

"It's a good place to talk as well. I've probably thought enough for today."

"So, you find magic here as well."

Hannah said nothing, for she had already answered the question as far as she intended.

"Have you seen any ghosts? Or anything spooky?"

"Mainly anglers. A few can be creepy, but not spooky. I've glimpsed fools looking for gold and once, but not today, one looking for old tombstones. He must have been high, but I directed him to the cemetery. The ghosthunters are spooky.

They haunt cemeteries you know, searching for phantoms. Its funny, the living haunting the dead. It's supposed to be the other way around."

"Looking for what?" Linda asked Hannah, but she could have easily posed the question to herself.

"I don't know. They had little time for the dead when they were upright and among us. In death they have been transformed in local celebrities. For nothing more than being dead."

"I'll take that as a no, you haven't seen any ghosts."

Hannah frowned in acknowledgement. This woman asked ridiculous questions.

"You don't believe in spirits?"

"I don't need to. I got a C in American history. Does that make it more or less true?"

Linda didn't see the logic and let Hannah's observation pass.

Maybe it was time to cut this conversation short. But Hannah had no special plans, she could endure social studies so why not one more additional waste of time.

Hannah visibly relaxed, causing Linda to wonder why the teenager had been so anxious. "Maybe it's me," she speculated.

"You could start a club, a business maybe, Linda" Hannah said abruptly.

"A business?"

"We have great freeway access. One billboard east and one for westbound traffic, GHOST HUNTERS, or something like that." She pointed with a movement of her head to the massive roadworks, echoing her earlier method of providing directions to the campers.

"You could tie it into the gold detectors and get some from overflow from Rose Hill."

"I've heard that name before. Who is she?"

"Who?"

"Rose Hill."

"Rose Hill is not a person, but a town. It's a psychic village about an hour east of Brentville. They believe in ghosts in a big way."

"I'm sure that they do. This sounds very interesting, but a new business is not for me."

You don't have to believe any of it. Who would really? Unless its your business, and then it would simply be business."

"Like professional sports teams."

"Exactly. You don't have to enjoy it."

Hannah saw that Linda was not convinced.

"My friend Emily doesn't believe in history but she got an A."

"I see," Linda responded, although she did not understand.

Hannah tried another argument.

"If you are going to remain in Brentville, then you must get involved. Or you will go nuts, without even realizing it."

36

"I'm retired."

"More involved than watching other people jump."

"People like yourself?"

Hannah nodded.

"I'm still retired."

"That doesn't matter. In fact, it provides you more opportunity."

Hannah took a breath and pressed on.

"You are too young to freeload".

"Is that what you think I'm doing?"

"What are you doing here?" Hannah asked, trying to hide the resentment that was building. This woman was just another variant of the anglers and detectors.

"I find Brentville magical. Brentville is so..."

"If you utter the word cute, I'll scream," Hannah cut her off, hiding her anger in a joke.

"Believe me, I can scream."

This woman was affluent, educated, and she had tossed it all away to move here.

"What did she know that had escaped Hannah's own analysis," the younger woman wondered.

"If you were so enamored with our past, where were you last year and the year before, of for that matter, the past last century?"

"My infatuation is recent."

"Why now? Were you simply passing through?" Hannah looked again to the overhead freeway, implying that road was still open for Linda to leave.

"Yes. I was simply passing."

Hannah was going to speak, thinking that Linda had finished, when the older woman continued in two-word bursts,

"En route, to my, to some, some future."

"That is so exciting," Hannah blurted, the rush a counterpart to Linda's slowing pace. This was better, a future. Maybe she had misjudged Linda.

"Some future, same future."

"And then you stopped here, tossing that future in the trash." Hannah could not hide her disappointment this time.

"These futures, the same. All futures, the same."

She looked at Hannah, not expecting confirmation. Clearly, her words were not resonating with the girl. "Why would they, she is not you," Linda thought.

"It must be an age thing, Hannah. I appreciate you listening to what must sound like defeat. I felt as if the future had run out of gas, here on the outskirts of this town. Brentville was as far as life was willing to carry me."

"How awful".

Linda laughed at Hannah's disgust.

"Your story would make more sense if you'd told me that you'd been abducted."

They both sensed that this conversation, so odd for what was really their first true encounter, had ended badly.

"Welcome to Brentville, Linda. I really hope that you enjoy it."

"Thanks. Me too. I hope to speak with you again. I'll choose a happier topic, the future perhaps."

"I'd enjoy that. I'll see you at GE."

"Giant Eagle," she added, seeing Linda's confusion.

CHAPTER EIGHT

Its sign read tearoom. In addition to tea, it sold frames and framing, artwork, and soaps and various salves, all displayed under track lighting set in the fourteen foot or so ceilings.

The establishment recalled art galleries in any big city but here the low rent permitted a larger space.

Narrow planks, light colored and installed diagonally completed the store, while music quietly filled the space. The choice of genre seemed to be accomplished by random selection.

It was a quiet spot in a quiet town, popular with retired and retiring teachers.

A mural on the ceiling served to disguise the fact that the room was taller than it was wide. The disparate elements combined to make a pleasant gathering place

The tearoom proprietor was speaking with her mother while Linda sat contentedly sipping her hot brew.

She felt herself a local but knew that it was only pretense. She'd heard of a woman in town for more than four decades, but not yet a native.

At a far table, a family of four was enjoying a snack. The younger daughter was permitted to stand on her chair while eating without being scolded. Too big for a highchair while too small and short to sit or to be corrected for her cute misbehavior.

The guard from the courthouse had stopped by on his way to work.

It was to be another slow day at the courthouse, there was absolutely nothing on that day, he was telling the owner and her mother. The proverbial slow wheels of justice were afforded a complete rest.

It was the slow season in the county, when warm weather and extended daylight distanced victim from victimizer

The guard would have a boring day, and the tearoom provided a chance to talk.

"What few trials we do get are reruns?"

"Like appeals?"

"No. The trials themselves are tedious and trivial. It's the same stupidity over and over. Ad nauseous. I learned that phrase from one of the attorneys."

"Even murder?"

"Murder is no exception. It's mundane."

"Did the same attorney teach you that word?"

"Yes," he answered, blushing in embarrassment.

"Murder is mundane," he repeated.

"It lacks imagination and meaningful motive. That is all me by the way," he said proudly.

"I'd rather be fishing and in the fresh air, sitting in a much softer seat than the unpadded wooden one I have to use, babysitting the worst folks in the county. But it pays well."

In a corner, an elderly man sat alone, confiding in his warm beverage. He carried a blue mask instead of a handkerchief in the breast pocket of his sports jacket. The mask sat there vertically, ready to defend against the next virus. It lingered as a fashion statement, one no more bizarre than another, mutated into a silk kerchief, always azure.

Linda recognized that the woman at the next table was in town for a funeral. She was too well dressed for a weekday, too relaxed to be working. She was morbidly fascinated to meet relatives of the deceased. They were vulnerable but strangely more alive, reduced in their focus of the world. What better place to hear an echo of the past than at a wake, or outside of a funeral home.

Linda had spoken to a few male mourners in the café, over the past several weeks, they had asked her for advice, directions, trivial information. She did her best to provide details on the town, feeling like an imposter.

It was unusual to speak with female grievers, although Linda hadn't developed a theory to explain it.

Perhaps women were used to handling loss and disappointment. Or maybe the loss was offset by relief, a feeling that it, whatever it might be, had finally ended, like an extended bad date.

Today however was an exception.

Ellie, Linda learned the woman's name a few minutes later, began the conversation.

"Are you local?", Ellie asked.

"More of less," Linda hedged. "How may I help you," she continued, five simple words that Zeke would have approved.

"I'm wondering about the theater," said the stranger.

"The theater?" Linda repeated, confused.

"The Columbia theater a few blocks down," the woman said, pointing vaguely down Main Street.

"Oh, yes," Linda replied.

"Is there a performance tonight or tomorrow?"

"Sorry, no there isn't."

"Too bad, I so enjoy theater."

"It used to be a movie theater, originally that it. Now it's a community theater."

"Are you involved with it?" queried Ellie, but she did not wait for response.

"If I lived in such a wonderful town, I would be. Everything is so quaint."

Linda smiled at the word, imagining Hannah howling in pain, and nodded in agreement. Maybe she should get herself more involved in local activities. Next week, or the week after.

Ellie continued her interrogation.

"What is your role in the theater?" she asked, having already assigned Linda more responsibility than she desired.

"Well," Linda began, searching for the least powerful lie to use.

"I'm..."

"I suspect that you run the entire theater, don't be modest."

Linda was tempted to look around to see if Zeke was nearby, if this was some elaborate gag. Instead, she remained focused on the stranger, not willing to give any prankster watching the satisfaction of her discomfort.

"Which lie to use?" Linda considered.

Ellie continued her spontaneous monologue, sparing Linda from deceit before the cocktail hour.

"Years ago, I was part of a theater group back home. In Louisville," she explained, and then added, "Kentucky. It was wonderful, I so enjoyed it."

The woman sipped from her coffee cup.

"I can be again, now that Dan is gone."

"Your husband?" Linda asked, providing Ellie a brief interval to inhale.

"Yes."

The late husband rated one final word.

"Yes," Ellie repeated.

Linda nodded, sensing instinctively that "I'm sorry" would have been excessive condolence.

"Theater is better than life," Ellie stated it in the same way that one is taught two plus two equals four.

Linda raised her eyebrows in unspoken question. She understood that in this small play, hers was to be mostly a silent part.

"You get to rehearse and relive the most interesting parts of life and discard the boring bits. And then there is the applause at the end."

Linda looked on encouragingly.

"I'm Ellie, by the way," the woman said.

"Linda".

"Its like this funeral."

Ellie paused, unsure if she should continue speaking to this stranger.

Linda recognized the hesitation; it was common to all genders. Yet it was easier to tell a stranger secrets. It was as if the bereaved was speaking to the wind on an early morning deserted beach. It would not actually be heard. Linda

42

remained silent, her stillness generating a vacuum primed to extract words from Ellie's closed mouth.

Another moment of silence passed, then Linda removed the last impediment.

"Like the funeral?" she asked innocently.

"I knew what to do. I've attended plenty of funerals at our, my age. I felt like an understudy who now had center stage. I knew by heart the role of widow, the dialogues and nuanced movements. It was to be a singular performance."

"And Dan, he really, well they say not to speak ill of the dead, but it is his living actions that I criticize. He was, oh Linda this will sound dramatic. But Dan was a villain. You, a person I mean, doesn't get to meet many villains. They are pretty rare, I think."

"You would be surprised," Linda thought, but she shrugged in response. "Yours is not a speaking role," she reminded herself.

"But now that he's gone, I have my future before me, it's incredibly exciting, but at the same time, more than a little frightening.

"I suppose that it is."

"But you won't have to deal with him, your late husband, Dan," Linda managed to remember.

"You described him as a villain."

"He was. But I just don't know where I'm going to find another one. Up to now, when I look back on it, my life was a series of auditions with rejection the sole verdict. It was a condensed version of disappointment."

"That's very pessimistic, Ellie."

"But now as a widow, I have one more tryout."

"Or more."

"Or more."

At that moment another woman entered the conversation.

"Excuse me for interrupting, but you need to get yourself to Rose Hill."

Ellie looked at Linda, who shrugged.

"I couldn't help but eavesdrop. It helps in my business. I'm Cassie."

43

Linda and Ellie regarded Cassie expectantly.

"I'm a nurse. Most days I work in the prison infirmary the other side of Rose Hill. I treat the breakers and the broken. Evenings I volunteer at the hospice on the outskirts of town. There, I work among the worn-out."

"Hospice," Linda thought with a shudder.

"It helps to listen to folks, sometimes especially if they resent it."

"You're local?" asked Linda.

"I live in Summerville."

"What is Rose Hill?" Ellie asked with a hint of impatience.

"It's a psychic village about thirty miles east of here," Linda explained.

"Yeah, but it is the place to find men," Cassie exclaimed.

One of my patients," Linda and Ellie assumed from hospice, but Cassie did not specify, "has a cousin, another widow, who told me all about it."

"She spends weekends over in Rose Hill. I thought that she was wasting money trying to contact her dead husband."

"Do people really do that?" Ellie asked.

"Sure. But not this woman. Her name is Annie. She told me that two weeks was long enough and that it was time to focus on the living. Karl didn't merit a long period of mourning."

"Karl?"

"Annie's late husband."

Linda felt that what had been a small two woman play moments ago, was on the verge of expanding into a cast of dozens. She wondered if she should begin to take notes. She glanced at Ellie, but instead of shock or annoyance at this stranger's cavalier talk of death, the fresh widow was enraptured with the story so far.

Cassie went on.

"Annie's cousin,"

"Your patient?" Linda asked, not wanting to get lost too soon.

"Yes. Well, she, Ruthie, the patient, tells Annie, her cousin, 'That's cold, Annie.'

44

'So is Karl, dear cousin. We both know that he was never hot stuff.'"

Linda and Ellie sipped coffee, while Cassie caught her breath.

"Ruthie says, "You've become cynical Annie. It becomes you. Cynicism is the perfect tint that goes so well with your natural color."

Cassie stopped for a moment to explain. "Annie is definitely not the most spiritual of people. Ruthie told me that she went to church every week because she lives in a small town, for the same reason that people set out their garbage bins every week; it's a good way to meet neighbors and it avoids raising a stink."

"We seem to be leaving the men out this conversation," Ellie observed.

"You're right. So, off she goes to Rose Hill, hosing money on something that she has no faith in, attempting to contact her late, mediocre at best husband, who if he did respond, would scream at her to stop spending his money frivolously.

"What is she doing in Rose Hill?" asked Linda, puzzled at Annie's action but pleased that she was still following Cassie's epic.

"The same thing any self-respecting widow would be doing; looking for a replacement."

"A replacement husband?"

"Ideally, it would be an upgrade. Of course the supply and demand ratio is not to her advantage, and she has to beware of widowers who have the same plan as her."

"Which is to find a decent, well-off number two?"

"Or three, or four. Annie told me that people invariably pose the same foolish questions to psychics, 'When will I die? Will I be rich?' They never ask, 'When will I live?'."

Ellie and Linda sat quietly.

"Rose Hill. A psychic village. Nevertheless, it's a good fishing hole. What do the young people call it? IRL. In real life."

"Do you think that she, this Annie, is really husband hunting? She's investing a great deal of money in what may be nothing."

"Not really. Only Annie knows how much money she spent on mediums. Its all cash, so..."

"I see," Ellie said slowly, and it was clear that she did indeed see something.

"She doesn't need to consult any psychics; she can just make up her own message from beyond and tailor it to each man she meets. Fortunately, she still has an excellent memory and won't tangle up her..."

"Lies? She won't mix up her lies to each man?" Linda protested.

"I was going to say lines, her numerous fishing lines."

"You call them lines; I call them lies."

"Oh, I don't know Linda," Ellie said soothingly.

"Fishing sounds like a wonderful hobby for a widow such as myself."

"If you land one worth keeping, you should move here."

CHAPTER NINE

A few Sundays later, Linda stopped at Giant Eagle to buy some plants and potting soil. And a small indoor planter, as she had delayed too long as it was. It was also a chance to talk to Hannah. She saw a lot of herself in the young woman. Maybe she could help. But first she herself would need assistance with her purchases.

"Hi Hannah."

"Hello. Still not bored? I made a bet with myself that you would be gone by today. I can't believe you chose to move to Brentville. There is nothing here."

"I was well informed."

Hannah did not pursue the cryptic response. Linda was still a mystery.

For her part, Linda was disarmed by Hannah's bluntness. It had been the same during their conversation in the park. She seemed to be in a hurry, despite moving with the energy saving motions of an athlete.

"Have you seen any ghosts?" Hannah joked.

"Not that I've noticed."

"I've been thinking about the business idea we discussed."

Linda hadn't thought that Hannah was serious.

"We must receive a certain amount of overflow from Rose Hill."

"Ghosts?" Linda laughed.

"With the B&B near the funeral home, it's only natural that we.".

"How do they pay, these spirits."

"Not them, Linda. Its people in general, they try to contact their deceased relatives since they are so close."

"Perhaps some of them do."

"I'm just saying that we get some interesting visitors."

"Present company included?"

"I'm not sure about you, not yet. You're a resident, maybe not quite a resident but more than a visitor."

"In your business then, I'm not a typical client, since I'm not a B&B guest contacting a ghost."

"No, not hardly. Besides, being down in a valley we have very poor phantom reception. We'd have to start our business uptown, where there is better traffic."

"I'm still retired, but we can talk about your future."

Hannah pounced on the offer.

"Absolutely. When?"

"Soon, in the next couple of days."

Hannah returned to the business at hand.

"Still no meat? You don't eat much."

"I guess not. Maybe gardening will perk up my appetite. I wanted to plant some flowers in and around the house. Do you know much about these?", pointing to the marigolds, which she had selected solely by the name.

"These are annuals."

"What does that mean? Is that good?"

"I have no idea. I read the label; see it says annual. They are pretty in any case."

"Could you help me carry all this stuff to my house, its just up on Snowden, by the Catholic church."

"I would if I could Linda, but I can't leave for two more hours. And then I need to rush to the diner. Sorry."

She looked around, and then said, "You are in luck. Mike is in the store."

"Who?"

"Mike Hayes, over there. He does odd jobs of all sorts. He is well suited to it."

"How is that?"

"Mike is odd. Not creepy, simply odd. He is another vegan, like you."

"I'm not," Linda protested, and then stopped herself. It didn't matter. Denials would lead to explanations and questions.

She didn't pry and did not like when others pried on her.

"I can talk to you," Hannah said, the words disconcerting Linda.

"Because I'm new in town."

"Because you are leaving."

The response chilled her. She wished that she was at home, a fire roaring in the hearth. She did not understand how this young, relative stranger knew. But she was the first to confirm her diagnosis.

CHAPTER TEN

"Are you two detectors?" Hannah asked the diners.

"Detectives?", one replied. Hannah would have had difficulty distinguishing one of the men from the other. In her experience, men over a certain age all looked the same.

"Sorry."

Hannah was disappointed that she had misjudged this pair. Usually, she was good at spotting detectors.

"I asked if you two were detectors, treasure hunters. You know, searching for hidden treasure with metal detectors.":

"No, we're not detectors miss," the other replied, his face still wearing a quizzical look."

"Is there treasure to be found around here?"

"No, none at all," Hannah wanted to say.

"Supposedly there is civil war lost gold in the area. The FBI was here a few years ago, trying to recover it."

"Did they?"

"Nobody knows. Or they haven't said. So..."

"These detectors are still searching?"

"Yep. Are you anglers?"

"Anglers? Oh, fishermen. No, not really. We are camping for a few days. We have a site reserved in Cook Forest."

"I hope that our RV fits," the other man said, pointing to a large motor home parked in front."

"If I see a deer," the first diner continued, "I will consider it a success."

"Some campers have spotted bears recently. They are quite active at this time of year."

The pair looked at Hannah as if she were an zoological expert.

"That would be something, wouldn't it, Norman?"

"A bear? Sure. But what about bars? Can you help us out there, Hannah?"

"There is a bar in town, but parking would be a problem, with that," her head moving to indicate their motorhome.

"Uber?"

Hannah laughed.

"Uber no. New York is 400 miles that way," her head again signaling direction.

"Maybe you could drive us?"

"That's an even bigger no, boys," Hannah said to the two men old enough to be her grandfather. Boys liked to be called men, and men boys. Another tip for tips, her mentor Millie had told her.

"I get better tips with 'honey' that I do with 'moron'," had been her first suggestion.

"I'm not old enough to drink."

"So much the better. We're too old to do much else. You are old enough to drive?"

"Yes."

"Then its settled."

Hannah laughed again, safe in the comfort of the café.

"I don't have a car."

She'd taken to lowering her age, saying that she was 17 was a foolproof way to dispose of fools, the older they were, the more rapidly they retreated.

Her bike gave credence to her subterfuge

The old guys ordered no dessert. "It cuts into the calories allotted to alcohol," Hannah thought.

Hannah considered the motorhome, but it would guzzle any money that she had been able to save. And then there were the dogs, they looked friendly, but the dogs belonged to the old guys.

CHAPTER ELEVEN

"Hannah was right about Mike Hayes, odd but not creepy," Linda concluded after the odd job man had left. He had carried to Linda's home the items that Linda was not able to manage alone: the potting soil and planter, and some of the marigolds. Like Linda, he had no vehicle.

He was knowledgeable about gardening, it had been a passion once, he had intimated during the short walk to Snowden address.

He proffered advice on the planting and care, and offered to help with any outside work she might need.

It was clear however that he would not enter the house. Linda recalled his refusal to enter the nearly empty diner the other week. Linda wondered if he thought her as odd as she thought him, although odd in this case was more a reticence combined with old world politeness. "Does the town see me similarly," she asked herself.

Mike noticed the piano in the house, and despite his obvious interest, that too was insufficient temptation to come into the house.

"If you need any other outside help, Linda, here is my cellphone number."

"Its funny Mike, but somehow I envisioned you without this modern convenience."

"Its convenient for clients, not for me. But it is what it is. I pick up whatever work that I can."

He didn't say until, but Linda sensed that there was definitely an until lurking in Mike Haye's life.

"Do you do any home repairs, plumbing, painting, things like that?"

Linda had no idea why see asked, already having decided that she was done with any renovation or repair that would disrupt the tranquility of her life. She would change lightbulbs and replace toilet paper, but aside from this home gardening chore that she needed to perform, she was more or less, no totally done with that.

"No, I don't. That sort of thing would keep me indoors, and..."

"I see," Linda said graciously.

"The man who does the electrical work in town also runs the water plant. He also doubles as a plumber with his brother-in-law."

"Do they do lawn work too?" Linda asked, half jokingly.

"That is their nephew."

"They manage that part of reality where all fantasies stop to recharge."

Linda looked at him quizzically.

"Fantasy beats reality until the stench of a stopped toilet intervenes. It is impossible to fantasize that odor away. It shows we aren't in charge."

"This man and his brother-in-law sound very busy, and important."

"Yes. They flit from scene to scene. They are what you might call first responders.

For the first time, Mike Hayes smiled, and said, "The nephew is the last responder."

"Lazy?"

"No, he isn't lazy. He digs the graves at the cemetery."

"And mows the lawn?"

"Yes, he does that too."

CHAPTER TWELVE

The Catholic church bell seemed extra loud this morning. She had missed during its recent confinement, and it had only two days ago been freed from its stuck condition. Making up for lost tolls, it was ringing joyfully this glorious Friday morning. It added its frenetic energy to the reveille of blue jays.

Yesterday had been surprisingly cold and wet, today was forecast to remain unseasonably cold and dry. The overcast would be a delightful change on her walk today.

Linda strode down to Taylor, passing a house where three pairs of pants had been hung that morning on a clothesline.

"I love this town," she said to herself. "Eden is inspirational, with or without God."

The town was picturesque in the way that comes from the result of an accommodating Nature aided by hard work and consistent maintenance. The effect was à work of art, a largish village lovingly painted in quaint.

Minutes later she reached the convenience store, where she purchased a bottle of water and a granola bar.

The store was small and catered to true locals. Its sister stood a mile or so away on the upper side. The upper side was anywhere USA, another ubiquitous freeway stop, a come and go shop with an unbelievable number of coffee pots. It was the Ohara of caffeine. The sheer number of pots in such a remote convenience store had nearly deterred Linda from her plans. Each burner with its steaming contents represented a certain number of people, pure noise and mayhem.

Fortunately, she had decided to stay and chanced to meet the man she thought of as a prophet. A misguided one, a compass that pointed due south.

She turned toward inspiration park, one of her self designated city gates.

Linda found no inspiration in the park, but then she had lost the taste for it since her installation in Brentville, as it required follow-up action. And she was retired if not tired.

Having reached the perimeter of her world, Linda turned around and scanned her home. There was a lot of life in these 2000 acres. It was a large convenience store, well stocked with everything a person could need. And more. The town was surprisingly full of interesting men, Linda thought.

"At least two," she assured herself.

As she crossed the bridge to Main Street, she stopped to search the park with her eyes.

The dog and his disk were nowhere to be seen, the man must work, Linda sighed.

CHAPTER THIRTEEN

Linda dreaded Wednesdays, the day of real-world work. Mail burning, and a simple review of the contents of the weekly FedEx package. One or two unavoidable phone calls or trips to websites. To reduce the drudgery of that day, she had scheduled with Mike to stop by to help with some chores, outside activities only, she had assured him.

She was grateful for Mike's phobia about entering empty buildings as she preferred to do the indoor planter herself. She had completed that chore early, then retrieved the mail and FedEx package. She had nearly gone through the correspondence at the kitchen table, rushing through with her soil-stained hands, anxious to finish before Mike arrived. The doorbell rang, damn, he might be odd, but he was punctual.

Linda and Mike were standing in her back yard.

She was glad, as she had always found it harder for people to lie when they were standing. Deception requires the support of a good chair.

This was too important to relate inside, relaxed on a recliner.

"What is your story, Mike?"

"You won't believe it."

"Do you believe it?"

"Some days I do, others I'm not so sure. Most days, I put it out of my mind."

Linda was curious enough to ignore Mike's stop sign.

"Believable stories are rarely worth listening to."

"Or telling. That is why children dislike school."

Linda pressed.

"I'm genuinely curious Mike, but if you don't want to talk about, well do it anyway."

Mike laughed at the directness.

"You're not shy, are you Linda?"

Receiving no response, Mike continued.

"OK, here goes. I've been in Brentville for over 18 months, so the events are beginning to fade. If I get some of the details wrong, I don't care. I'd be just as happy to remember none of them."

Do you use cannabis?" He asked.

"What? No, I don't," Linda babbled back, flustered by the question.

"But if you feel the need, for some grass, marijuana," Linda sputtered

"No, I don't take drugs, I was asking to see if you knew what the term meant."

"Oh, sure," Linda said, her voice calming.

"You see how you misunderstood? Something similar but much more sinister happened to me. I was dating this wonderful woman, Amelia. I thought that we would marry. One evening, over dinner in a noisy, crowded restaurant, she told me that her family was into cannabis in a big way, it was a religion.

'Cannabis,' I repeated silently to myself. Who was I to judge? Tolerance I came to understand, can be a dangerous and near fatal weakness, and not the universal virtue that its adherents proclaim."

"Hmmm," Linda murmured.

"'So, her family enjoys a little weed,' I continued my internal dialogue. Weed, cannabis, Maryjane, grass, the object itself had more aliases than a lifelong criminal. Smoking the dried leaves was not a predilection that one bragged of, but neither was it a crime, not a real crime that is."

Mike looked at Linda, pausing for comment. Linda said nothing.

"I did not discover my mistake until a few weeks later at one of Amelia's family gatherings, several counties over. It was indescribable. I had to flee."

"To Brentville?"

"To anywhere. It was Brentville by chance. I fled the 'party'.

I drove, so fast, it was late, no destination in mind, no mind, I think. I was exhausted, any adrenaline had long since dissipated, and then. I saw the sign for Brentville. I took the first exit and ended up at the B&B on Main. I didn't want to park my car at any of the freeway hotels."

"In case," Linda began.

"Yes."

Mike took a moment to breath.

"It was late as I said, but fortunately the Barnier house had a vacancy, a cancellation, I often wondered later who that cancellation had been. Its silly, but I thought somehow that it was important."

"I see."

"The following morning, I noticed the serenity of the town."

"I know what you mean," Linda echoed.

"And I saw the Odd Fellows engraving on the building. I misunderstood what it was and decided to stay another day. That was 18 months ago."

"I see."

"I'm not sure that you do Linda."

"Cannibals and not cannabis was what my lovely Amelia had actually said."

Linda felt that it was her to turn to speak, to relate a confidence, one refuge to another.

"I'm ill, very ill, but none of these medical professionals have been able to find anything wrong."

"Wrong with you?"

"Yes, nothing. They haven't found a damn thing." She paused. "But I've found plenty wrong with them."

Linda reached into her purse and pulled out a newspaper clipping.

"Here, read this."

"This is very sad. Oh, wait, is this yours? You were sick? As a young girl?"

"No, it's not me. Notice the date. It's from a month ago. She's certainly dead now. That doctor of hers though, that is the sort of physician that I need. One who isn't blind, or mute. One who can tell a woman as readily as a girl that she is dying."

Mike looked again at the clipping and reread it silently, before passing it back to Linda.

Hi Everybody

Doctor Kathy asked me to write the letter. I don't understand why. She said it was important.

Doctor Nieden said it was ok for me to call her Kathy.

I'm dying. It hurts most of the time.

Is this enough Doctor Kathy? I hope so. I'm tired.

I like Doctor Kathy. She takes care of me.

Bye now.

Morgan.

PS

Love
Morgan.

After Mike left, Linda returned inside, finally washing the grime from her hands. She washed and washed, the warm water providing her with sound and sensation to reflect.

She had the luxury of time. For a while. Time was a richness more valuable than money. But then, she possessed that too in large quantity.

She watched her money, then she had hired multiple levels of pseudo trustworthy accountants to suspect each other and protect her money.

Linda regretted not being able to do the same with her time. It was luxurious, her glorious days, but they were numbered.

The pseudo medical professionals were unanimous in their verdict, but they had to be unanimously wrong. She would not believe them any more than see would believe any one of her money managers.

She had plenty of money, experts said. She had plenty of time, other experts had proclaimed.

So, she had bought gold, and brought it with her to this town, where the past held sway, where she might in fact have more time, the best of luxuries.

And she still had plenty of money, experts said. They confirmed it each Wednesday by courier. ·

"Plenty of money", she scolded herself.

She had the luxury of time, for a while. It was wonder, exquisite, addictive beyond belief, fatal beyond refute.

Maybe in Brentville, she could escape from time, for what was the future but time.

She felt as if she could regard the sun, high in her sky, and command it to halt just for her. It was fruitless, the golden star moved annoyingly across the blue.

She would bend the star to her will, if not today, tomorrow or the day after that.

Soon, it mattered not when, for she had the luxury of time, for a while.

Linda thought of Mike Hayes. It was obvious that he saw things that weren't there. His story of a cannibalistic girlfriend was ridiculous. It was positively Freudian, as was his fear of entering buildings with fewer than seven people. There too he suffered from visions, some private intense phobia. Another delusional person.

"But so are you," a voice mocked.

Was Mike Hayes completely mad?

"Are you?" the snide voice echoed.

Linda had to agree. She and Mike shared something in common. They were convinced of their own truths, confident in their faiths.

He feared a flesh-eating monster, a beast so well disguised that his fear was not to be believed. She had her own, one that even this minute was consuming her brain in a matter that no doctor could detect.

Mike had not refuted her statement. He must have agreed with her. She should have asked him. She needed a doctor who could see what others said was not there. She would settle for a gardener with that same gift."

The radio weatherman had spoken of a late season frost overnight. It made her feel like a farmer, listening to weather as she did each day. There was no traffic report of consequence.

Linda enjoyed chopping wood purely because she was so poor at it. She especially enjoyed the part about not slicing off a finger or a foot, for which neither did she have any spares. The swing of the sharp blade kept her mind focused. Now this was a chore worthy of the name, she thought. As she carried an armful into the living room there was a knock at the front door. Linda dropped the cut wood onto the hearth, relishing the sound made by the tumbling oblong pieces as they smacked each other and then the fireplace bricks. One struck the toe of the old, oversized steel toed boots that she wore, a welcome gift left by the former occupant. That impact was more of a thud and signaled the finale of the impromptu concert. Linda opened the door to find Zeke and his niece Emily.

"Hello Linda. I would have called except I don't have your number."

Linda smiled, for this was a line that she had not heard before. But it was true, no one had her number, and she kept the phone only for the increasingly little amount of work that she had to do online.

"Let me introduce my niece, Emily Parks. Emily, this is Ms. Linda Smith."

"I saw you race weeks ago. You were great."

Emily blushed at the compliment.

"Thanks Mrs. Smith," Emily replied.

"Please accept this book as a welcome to Brentville," Emily continued, passing a wrapped parcel to Linda.

Emily's voice held the long rural vowel sound common to the area, a remnant from immigrant ancestors.

Zeke spoke again.

"Emily wanted to see the house, and, like I said, I didn't have your telephone number. Instead of stopping by to ask for your number just to return home and call you to ask if we could stop by, well that seemed a bit foolish and you might get the wrong idea about me asking for your number, and you might say no, to either giving me your number or to us stopping by."

"Please take a breath Zeke."

Emily spoke while Zeke inhaled.

"I really do want to see the house and what you've done with it, Mrs. Smith."

"I'd be delighted, Emily, but the entry fee for this private tour, is for you to call me Linda, and not Mrs. Smith. As far as I know, there is no Mrs. Smith in this house. There is a Ms. Smith, but she goes by Linda as well."

"Linda," Emily echoed.

"You may be disappointed in the tour itself. To date, the only work I've had done is painting the upstairs bathroom."

Emily and Linda began to mount the stairs.

"I'll stay downstairs, if you don't mind. I'll make us coffee."

Linda turned slightly and joked, over her shoulder, "If you can cook, you can stay overnight."

"Vegan?" Zeke asked, but Linda had already turned away.

"We won't be long. Maybe Emily should give me the tour."

A short time later, Zeke heard a squeal and came hurriedly from the kitchen in time to see Emily sliding down the banister, with Linda frozen in place at the top of the landing, open mouthed.

Linda was tempted to slide down banister as Emily had just done with a guilt-tinged laugh.

"I hope you don't mind, Linda," she said after the fact.

"Mrs. Dietz used to let me, ever since I was a little girl."

"You still are," Linda thought.

"I don't mind at all; I've been tempted myself. Maybe later, when I'm alone," she said with a wink.

"I smell coffee."

"Let me get it", Emily said, dismounting gracefully and scurrying off to the kitchen.

"I apologize Linda. If I had known," Zeke began, approaching Linda and touching her shoulder.

"If I had known, I'd have asked you to take a photograph. There is nothing to apologize for, Zeke. Girls will be girls, at any age."

A few moments later, Emily returned with coffee.

"What do you think of the bathroom?"

62

"The bathroom is so much brighter than it used to be. Its very happy. I think that its great."

"Thanks."

"Are you planning other renovations, Mrs. Smith?"

"Its Linda, Emily, upstairs and down. No, I don't think so. Don't worry, I won't alter this a bit," caressing the smooth wood. It will be here waiting for you whenever you visit. Maybe your uncle will try it sometime."

The banister was exquisite, smooth, and polished. It's wide cross-sectional curve, classic and yet post modern in design. It accompanied the descent of the stairs like a comforting friend. But it was too wide, too smooth, too exquisite. In the case of a fall, it would remain stationary, too broad to grasp, too sleek to clasp. She would fall the length of twenty-four steps. Had that been the fate of the previous occupant?

"Beauty is chased, wrapped in danger."

"What's that?"

"Nothing. A fragment of poetry I must have read somewhere."

"Are you a poet, Linda?" Emily asked.

"No, not yet. But that is an idea."

"Poetry is my favorite class, next to track. It seems to have no purpose, which makes it special. And teachers can't really grade it. I used to go to inspiration park to write, but Brentville is one giant poem."

"I'm beginning to appreciate that benefit, it's not listed in the visitor's guide."

"You are not a visitor," Zeke stated.

"I am not a visitor?"

"Not a typical one. You an observer, if you are lucky, one day a resident."

He sensed that he had overstepped a line that only she could see.

"Or not. Still, you are a rare visitor. Not odd, just unusual."

"I will settle for that, a rare visitor. Who knows, as you say, one day a resident. Perhaps" she concluded with a smile, the under line transformed into an upward curve.

"Tell me, though" Linda said hesitantly.

"There are so many churches in town. Eight or so within a two-mile radius, but only one state building, the county courthouse. They can't all be right."

"They aren't, they're separated."

"I'm referring to all the different churches. How can one be valid and the other ones not?"

"Who said that?" Zeke asked, perplexed.

"Well, then why not have just one building?"

"Baskin-Robbins has dozens of flavors."

"You're being flippant Zeke Parks. That is not an answer."

"How can you say that? So does Dil's. Plus, they have black raspberry. How many times have you been to Dils?"

"A few," Linda admitted.

"Seriously, if God can't be all things to all people, who can? No one, he said," answering his own question.

Linda was not convinced.

"It's a healthy sign, there is something in God for everyone. As long as we tolerate each other's taste, we can all enjoy ice cream," Emily explained.

"This small town contains variety in abundance, open your eyes and enjoy. Especially the black raspberry, its seasonal you know."

The house felt empty. Tonight was filled with firsts. The innocent touch of Zeke, her joy at the sight of Emily's childlike behavior, and now the sense of being alone, in a house of which she had been the single inhabitant for over a month. How long has it been exactly, she asked the fire, her only companion, well dressed in blue and orange.

Maybe the coffee was making her jittery, a caffeinated part of her brain suggested. Another part agreed and recommended wine as cure.

She poured herself a glass of an earthy Pinot and selected a book from the numerous tomes left by the previous owner in the built-in bookshelves. The shelving was wood, as had been the book in a previous existence.

"Wood and more wood," she said aloud to the fire. The fire nodded in agreement, it too loved wood.

She was a normal patient, normal in her desire to have a superior doctor, a worker of if not miracles, then capable of one for her. She had gone to numerous physicians, hoping that one held a winning raffle ticket, and that they would confirm her illness. She neither demanded nor expected a cure, but surely a disease was on offer. How hard could it be? She was terminal, she knew it beyond unreasonable doubt. It was the learned medical professionals who were unreasonable in withholding their concurrence.

The previous occupant of the house had filled the bookshelves with mysteries and romances.

"Two sides of the same coin," Linda thought, selecting one at random. She read for a while, but the book held no interest. The flames presented more attractive diversion.

The fire was a wonderful conversationalist, crackling and waving wildly at her jokes, listening without criticism, forcing no advice.

As the night wore on and they both felt themselves fatigued, their discussion was reduced to whispers and eventually to warm silence.

Linda rose early the next morning. It was impossible to sleep when the sun was calling, despite the two glasses of wine the night before.

Her sleep had been without dreams. She remembered her dialogue with the living room fire. It had been delightfully pleasant. Maybe if her waking hours were crazy enough, she could avoid the arrival of nightly dreams.

She descended the stairs, nearly sliding down instead of walking, but any effects of the two alcoholic drinks had dissipated as she slept

She picked up the wine bottle and realized from the level of the remaining liquid, that she had consumed three glasses of the Californian Pinot, not two.

She felt fine, great, as Emily would say.

Another glorious day beckoned.

CHAPTER FOURTEEN

Later that day, Zeke was again at Linda's door.

"I still don't have your phone number."

"I would give it to you, but I don't remember what it is."

"I see," Zeke replied.

"I'm serious. I have no idea what it is. I hate phones. I only have one for emergencies," Linda explained in a half truth as she only had it for business.

"That is a sort of emergency," she rationalized to herself.

"I keep it turned off almost all of the time. I find that it renders the weapon safe, like keeping the chamber empty in a gun. I'm less likely to hurt myself with it. But if you really want it, I'll write it down when I turn the phone back on. It may be a while."

"Actually, I prefer stopping by. To that point, I'm following up on yesterday's date," he joked.

Linda didn't know how to respond, so she said nothing.

"And to apologize again for Emily."

"There is no apology needed. You don't know how close I came to replicating her slide, especially after a glass of wine last night. Or several."

"If you do decide to indulge let me know, I'll come over and cheer you on."

"Indulge in the banister or the wine?"

"Either."

"Your niece seems to know this house better than I do."

"That's Emily. She is the heir apparent to Brentville."

"In what way is that?'

"She could be the town's unofficial historian and its youngest, most fervent booster. Emily knows everything, I'm not an historian, of this town or any other. You need the right degree for that."

"Who says so?"

"Those with the requisite degrees."

"Doesn't your law degree count?"

"Negatively, I've been led to believe."

"Some folks just don't like attorneys."

Linda paused before adding, "I'm not some folks."

"That is excellent news. As far as local history, I enjoy it, but it's a passion with Emily."

"What about Hannah Faulor? Is she as knowledgeable as Emily?"

"Possibly, but I doubt it. You'll have to ask her yourself."

"What is her story, anyway?"

"Asks the local queen of mystery."

"So?"

"I'm not the town gossip either."

"Do they have degrees for that?"

He smiled

"Maybe. You will have to contact the historical society yourself. It would be a good icebreaker. You have lived in town long enough to start contributing."

"If you had difficulty, I'm sure that I'd never pass the background check. They might burn me at the stake. It would certainly give them some kindling on me."

"Really? Where there is fire there used to be smoke?"

"I'm taking the fifth."

"That's not fair. The society does a lot of wonderful things for the town, and they are often taken for granted. They need good people."

"Undoubtedly."

"Not everyone has led the exciting life that you have."

"What makes you say that?"

"I know many of the members."

"No, I mean about me."

"Things I've noticed, evidence, you might say. On the other hand, you might be surprised. Some of us have seen the outside world."

"Speaking of evidence, I see that you've Emily's gift in pride of place."

"Stone Church in the Wood," its an interesting title. I haven't had time to read it."

"It was written by Sheriff Arthur. I forget his last name, oh yeah that's right, Poplin," Zeke said, referring to the cover again. You'd think that I'd remember that name."

"Why's that?"

"I used to do some legal work for his son's company. The father and son were so unlike each other, that it was difficult to think of them sharing the same last name."

"When he retired, that was decades ago, he wrote that book. He took the photographs as well if I remember correctly. It would not surprise me to discover that the paper its printed on came from Buck's trees. That would be ironic, in a way."

"In what way?"

Zeke appeared to have not heard the question.

"Which company is that?"

"Buck's Lumber. It's not the most imaginative of names. If you haven't guessed, it's a logging company. We have quite a few of those in the area."

"Is it the one on White?"

"No, another one. His office is on the outskirts of the city."

Linda smiled at the way described Brentville as if it were a metropolis.

Zeke paused and regarded Linda for a long moment before continuing.

"He talks to trees."

"What? Oh, you mean like one of those environmentalists."

"They talk back to him. According to Buck."

"What is the punchline? You aren't joking?"

"No." He looked quietly at Linda, searching for any expression.

"I should have kept my lips sealed. I'm not a gossip. This is common knowledge that most people choose to ignore or forget. He doesn't advertise this, uh ability, not that he ever did. But he is more reticent about discussing it. He has a business to run, and employees who depend on it, and on him."

68

"Why tell me this, Zeke?"

"I don't know. To spare him, or you, embarrassment. So, if you speak with him.".

Zeke's attention returned to the book. He bent down and lifted it from the coffee table, weighing it in his right hand, as if it's worth could be measured by its mass.

"Arthur wrote this after his retirement as sheriff of Rose Hill.

It was strange doings. Whatever occurred happened before his retirement. Buck's girlfriend at the time, well she died. People claim that they don't enjoy gossiping, but they are willing to listen, and more than willing to offer corrections, however incorrect, when I recount the true version."

"The true version?"

"True to me. It is similar to your weekly newspaper here. Between the facts themselves, the reporter, and the editor, how much is lost in translation?"

"How much?" Linda asked sincerely.

"Correct." Zeke smiled.

"So, the sheriff left policing and six months or a year later this book appears. Apparently, he had enough of Hell and so he went looking for gods or ghosts, like most of us, I reckon."

"Interesting. Did he find either?"

"You can read the book yourself."

"No spoiler for me?"

"I doubt it. I mean I doubt that he found either. Other than carved stone and pretty windows, do either exist? Outside of the cool, numbing gloom of the buildings, the ideas melt pretty quickly."

Linda reflected on her own philosophy.

Relationships and understanding and self esteem, all of that self directed garbage that outdistanced any religion. It encouraged self appointed deities. The world was overfull of them.

Linda fanned through the book, the churches were fascinating, gorgeous, art in stone and glass, immense jewels that bedazzled.

"You've seen ours?"

"Ours?"

"The ones here in Brentville."

"No, not yet. From the outside, yes, of course. And I've heard them."

"Well once you do step inside, if you stay here long enough."

Linda said nothing, forcing Zeke to continue.

"After you view ours, you could visit several found in Arthur's book. They aren't far from here."

"I don't have a car."

"I find that odd."

"Not creepy?"

"I don't associate that word with you, Linda. I thought that you were a native born American, so you must have a car."

"I am, but I don't."

"You're not from New York, are you?"

Linda shook her head.

"How can you not have a car?"

"I just don't."

"Where are you from, Linda?" Zeke asked, suddenly serious.

"I live right here in Brentville, your honor," Linda joked.

"Ok, I won't press. I do. Have a car, that is I could take you," Zeke offered, and then quickly backtracked when he perceived her resistance

"Not a date, your honor, just something to do, a field trip. I have the perfect place in mind."

"I don't travel anymore."

For a reason that later he was unable to explain to himself, Zeke persisted.

"Being driven thirty miles on outback Pennsylvania roads is not traveling. For most of us, that would be a doctor's visit.

It's a day trip, if you decide to not do the Cross tour."

"The Cross tour? Is that what they call it?"

"It's my term. Do you think that I could copyright it?"

Zeke was serious and was surprised but then pleased to hear Linda's laugh.

"That sounds like yes to everything."

"No Zeke Parks, it is not a yes. It is a weak maybe."

70

"Is that weak as in not strong or as in seven days."

"Ask me again in a week."

CHAPTER FIFTEEN

Mike Hayes stopped by the following week, to check on the plants in the back yard.

"Linda, I see that you have the Stone Church book," he said, indicating the copy that lay on the patio table, next to a half empty glass of lemonade.

"It was a gift from Emily Parks."

"That Emily is a real sweetheart."

"Its funny that you have that book, as I wanted to talk to you about something."

"Sure, I have time now. Let me get you a glass of lemonade as well."

A moment later, Linda returned, passing the cool beverage to Mike, who sat, then stood up again a moment later when Linda remained standing.

"I've been meaning to discuss this with you for a while, Linda,' Mike began.

Linda tensed, concerned where this might be going.

"You've been in Brentville only a short time, but I've seen you all over town, talking to everyone, walking, attending events."

Linda held her breath, still unsure where Mike was headed.

"But," he paused and took a sip, the tinkle of ice cubes the only sound.

"This is very good."

"But?"

"But you are alone."

"I like being alone."

"I can see that, but there can be more"

Linda decided to end whatever this was before it went any further.

"I'm not looking for a boyfriend, Mike."

72

"What? Oh. OK. That's good to know. I guess."

"But."

"Really Mike, I'm not interested."

"In what? You haven't heard my proposal."

"A proposal is exactly what I am not interesting in hearing. I'm not looking for a boyfriend."

"Ok. I heard you the first time."

He paused for a long moment, then smiled.

"I'm not looking for a girlfriend, Linda. Its not that sort of proposal."

Linda blushed, and gulped the rest of her lemonade, swallowing one of the small ice cubes that remained.

"My proposal means you getting more involved in Brentville and the surrounding area, more than simply as an observer. I've been in Brentville for eighteen months. Getting involved in building, preserving this town has been the best thing for me in a long time. I'm here to ask for your support."

"Politics?" Linda asked incredulously. "I'm not political."

"Neither am I. It isn't that type of support."

Mike Hayes smiled and then continued explaining his plan.

"I'm considering making this a real tour, pointing again to the book. A regular event, you know, with flyers, a van, a website. Everything. Le Tour des Croix. The Tour of Crosses. It sounds better than the tour of rocks. Beginning and ending here in Brentville.

Linda's noncommittal hmmm was all the encouragement that Mike needed.

"I can do more than odd jobs".

"God jobs?" Linda asked teasingly, relieved that there had been no kneeling and ring ceremony to squash.

"There are worse careers."

"Why me?"

"Well, you seem to have a certain business sense, and you don't have that periodic crazy look like my one-time girlfriend had, and others have when they let their guard down," he said, after a pause.

"And others?"

Mike nodded slowly.

"Like who?"

"Hannah."

Linda burst out laughing.

"Hannah Faulor?"

Mike said nothing.

"Hannah?" persisted Linda.

"You haven't noticed?"

"Noticed what?"

"That girl is bad news."

"She must hide it well."

"She does indeed."

He paused, disappointed that his proposal had taken a detour, but this was important.

"At first, I thought that Hannah was odd, not creepy. I wish for her sake that she had stopped at creepy."

"She is eighteen."

"People are at their worst at eighteen. They have to age into goodness."

"This is the same Hannah that works at GE, right?"

"Yes, Linda. She has that same look of controlled crazy that I've seen."

"Where? In me?"

Linda was more than a little disappointed, when Mike replied, "No, not you," shaking his head emphatically. "Too bad," Linda thought "controlled crazy could be good look once in a while."

"Maybe I'm overly sensitive to..." not finishing his thought.

Linda's mind went back to the other week, when Mike accepted her crazy rambling at face value.

"Hannah is crazy, as dangerous as a polite, attractive cannibal. Or so says my new doctor," Linda reflected

She considered for a moment longer, then decided.

"Tell me more about your plan for this tour."

"My idea is to base the business here in Brentville. We already benefit from the interstate traffic, heck, you're here, aren't you?"

"Yes, I am here."

"I could piggyback off our being a destination. It would be good for Brentville. You could be my first client. It would be good for you, a way to jump into the community."

"Except that neither of us have a van," he said sheepishly.

"I need a partner, Linda."

Linda blushed again at the passion in his voice."

"Let me speak to someone about your plan."

"Someone?"

"A friend. I have a feeling that my friend would be very interested."

"Sure," Mike exclaimed, his voice rising.

"That would be fantastic."

Linda blushed even more, saddened to see no disappointment in Mike's eyes in her not being his partner.

After Mike had left, she went inside, leaving the back door open. It was a beautiful summer day, but Linda felt tired and cold.

She sat. She was tired. All of these unexpected demands for her time and attention. She had left that behind in the future that now seemed to be drawing near again. She was tired. She was cold.

The sun shone brightly in the clear sky, the outside warmth slid in through the door to the garden. It was too early for a fire, she was tired, and the fire would demand attention.

She stood and paced for a while. In lieu of a fire, she rubbed her hands together. Linda reached to the hook on the wall behind the still open door, retrieved a button sweater and tossed it across her shoulders like a cape.

Mike's plan, so similar to Hannah's. Gods and Ghosts were inescapable, even by a heathen like her.

She mounted the stairs, and crawled into bed, fitting a silk sleep mask over her eyes. She remembered that she had neglected to close the back door, but she was tired. She slept.

CHAPTER SIXTEEN

Emily woke without pain, without worry. Aside from minor soreness after the first day of track, she had known neither sort of anguish.

She stretched, warm beneath the lightweight quilt, perfect for the cool air of the high summer nights. The window of her upstairs bedroom was opened wide, the mesh screen screening mosquitoes but not the chant of frogs to which she had fallen asleep.

She slipped into fresh clothes, then brushed her teeth. Showering could wait until this evening.

Emily decided to skip her run and laughed at the phrase. She would walk her route today, and in those places where she would not be too noticed, she would in fact skip. She would skip like a schoolgirl, one much younger than her 17 years.

Thirty minutes later, as she passed the home that Linda was renting, Emily stopped and considered her next action. She thought still of the home as the Dietz house. The roses that Mrs. Dietz had tended so well were showing signs of her absence. Were roses able to grieve, or were they confined to only feeling joy?

Linda was not Mrs. Dietz, Emily told herself and moved off in a shuffle.

Emily was 17, a woman in many other cultures, but here in Brentville, she was still a child. She smiled and began to skip.

A few blocks later, her thoughts returned to the newcomer. Again, Emily stopped. Linda was distant, a difficult feat in Brentville. But she was trying to fit in, Emily admitted.

"Having Hannah helps," Emily said aloud.

"But soon she too will be gone, like Mrs. Dietz."

She had known both of them her entire life, forever. For seventeen years.

And uncle Zeke. Surely, he would not leave. Hannah had not been the only town's person to remark on Uncle Zeke and Linda. She had noticed it herself but took comfort in the knowledge that the stranger would find it impossible to stay, and Zeke would conclude that it was impossible to leave. Maybe they were just too old to see the truth of their circumstances.

It would turn out fine, everything would be great. Emily skipped the remainder of the route, gay as a rose.

Emily stopped by one day to say hello to Linda. A visit from Emily was never an interruption, she brought as much brightness to the downstairs as the renovation did to the upstairs bath.

Linda brought lemonade from the kitchen, and found Emily standing before the city map that Linda had mounted on the living room wall.

"I see that you've kept the old one as well, Linda."

"They're not much different. I'm glad."

"Me too. These railroad tracks on the old map, they no longer exist. The rails were torn up and sent as scrap to China years ago. All that is left is a bicycle path where folks can ride their bicycles made in China from recycled Brentville steel."

Emily stated it matter of factly, without bitterness.

"This new map shows them as stitches left behind from that operation."

Linda considered again asking Emily to accompany her on one of her daily walks but reached the same conclusion as before. It was better to keep separate the two Parks in her life

And separate they were, so different one from the other. Zeke was quiet, serious in a way that was anathema to Emily. The girl was perky, spunky, a joy to be with and to have around. Moreover, she loved Brentville in the deep way that only natives could. And she loved her boyfriend, who was Emily level great.

"I'm in no hurry to marry," Emily said innocently. "A year or two from now is fine."

Linda could not repress a smile and turned towards the marigolds to hide her bemusement.

"These flowers are doing well, much better than I could have anticipated. I'm not a total black thumb."

"Mrs. Dietz preferred roses, but she lived here for ages. They might need..." Emily's voice trailed off.

"The roses?"

Emily nodded

"They need attention?"

Emily nodded again.

Linda had considered calling Mike Hayes to look at the roses, he had even mentioned their condition once or twice. She was glad now of her inaction.

"Do you know much about roses? Would you like to help with their attention?"

Fortunately, both questions were answerable in the affirmative, and the girl's head continued to nod, like one of those old, bobble headed dogs from the 1960s that Linda had seen for sale in the Main Street antique shop.

"Stop by whenever you like, Emily. Roses are beyond my gardening ability, I'm afraid. They deserve better than me."

The subsequent smile on Emily's face brought one to her as well.

"You knew Mrs. Dietz very well; I hope that we can have something similar.

I understand that she has dementia."

Emily nodded slightly.

"My mother had dementia. It was not pleasant. A sense of time is needed to stay afloat in this ocean of life. Maybe you could take some of the roses to her."

Emily beamed.

Further discussion of affairs botanica was terminated by the arrival of Emily's Uncle Zeke.

"We make an odd trio: a young maiden, a middle-aged bachelor, and what?" Linda thought.

"What am I? Not an old maid, what was the term for a widowed divorcee? Surely not single? Divorced or widowed, synonyms for alone."

"Ready?" Zeke said.

Before Linda could think of an answer, Emily spoke.

"Yes, I'm ready. I have to leave now, Linda. Work, you know."

And with that, they were gone, the question still echoing in Linda's head.

"Ready?"

Linda envied Emily. It was not only her youth, not simply her optimism, but her ability to love. To love her boyfriend, whoever that was, this house, the roses of Mrs. Dietz. Linda had long ago exhausted her own supply; it was dead as the roses would be if not for the girl's care.

At a certain point, one runs out of love. Perhaps it would regenerate here in Brentville, with Zeke. "Or you may just be delusional," a silent voice suggested.

CHAPTER SEVENTEEN

The napkin slid from Yellowstone's lap and fell to the floor. "Damn gravity, they have is set too high in here," he cursed. He had finished his burger moments before, and the empty plate had been cleared away. He sat alone at the bar, nursing his beer.

He was running through the plot of his new novel in his mind. It was work, a hard lie. He had to keep track of each preceding falsehood. Invariably he would overlook one and the entire structure would begin to collapse. It reminded him of the home renovations that he had had done in the past, it was always more complex than first envisioned.

He missed the white noise of the conversations of strangers. The bar was empty except for himself and the young bartender.

She was short, petite, lithe came to mind, as if she had been turned on a lathe, all extraneousness removed by a craftsman. She was in better shape than he had ever enjoyed.

He watched the young woman behind the bar. She kept hitching up her tight jeans while he said nothing, but silently rooted for gravity, which was set too low after all, he decided.

A couple entered the bar and took a table. Yellowstone watched as the bartender stepped from behind the counter and walked over to take their order.
"Maybe gravity would be stronger in the middle of the room," Yellowstone hoped.

The man had a strange laugh. With his eyes closed, the sound struck Yellowstone as that emitted by a dog, a Labrador, he judged.

The scarf around his neck Yellowstone assigned as a collar.

Across the table the woman's scent wafted to his nostrils, perfume accentuated by perspiration.

The man spoke with his entire body. Yellowstone could not make out the words, but it could have been an argument, a bawdy illustrated joke, on an instructional chair yoga class. Only the man was familiar with the rhythm.

His movements were jerky, as if he were subject to the illuminated effects of a daytime strobe light. For some reason, his movements aggravated Yellowstone, who was torn between fleeing and calling 911, requesting a defibrillator.

Fleeing was out of the question, as he was waiting for someone.

Across the table from the agitated man, his young companion employed only her tongue, teeth, and splayed right hand., like a dental student moonlighting as a sign language instructor.

Yellowstone turned to face away from the couple, wishing that she would arrive soon.

Linda had agreed to meet Zeke for a drink in the downstairs bar of the café. She had abandoned the habit of being fashionably late, as that notion had always struck her as forcing her to be the one to wait.

She sat down a few stools away from the only other occupant, a middle-aged man with a small moustache and overly large wire rim glasses. He wore a silver and turquois bracelet around his right wrist, while a silver watch encompassed his left.

The man glanced at her, while Linda glanced at her Baume Mercier watch. She was fifteen minutes early, and wondered if she should sell the watch. What need of it did she have.

Linda ordered a club soda from the twenty something bartender and then looked around at the bar. It was decorated with the heads of mounted animals and beer signage. There were a few tables for diners who preferred a bit of privacy, and two booths. Comfortably rural.

"You must be Linda Smith."

Linda nodded at the man who had spoken and smiled pleasantly.

"I'm Jerry, but most folks call me Yellowstone. Zeke told me that two of you were meeting here, and I seized the opportunity to make your acquaintance. We used to work together."

"As attorneys?"

"Yes. But that was years ago, I've only recently moved back to Brentville."

"From Yellowstone?"

"No, from out west yes, but not Yellowstone. The town hasn't changed much since I left. Culligan moved from one end of town to another, that confused me at first. And the old Jefferson manor was gone. But that was about it."

The places he mentioned were meaningless to Linda but nevertheless she nodded in agreement.

"What brought you back to Brentville?" Linda asked, hesistant to add his nickname to her question.

"I could say a car, but that wouldn't answer your question. Weariness and family."

"And you?"

"Maybe weariness as well."

"Now that I am back, I'm not sure if it is where I belong." Jerry halted, then continued.

"I'm here now. When I look back on it, my past is a set of randomly arranged former presents, like an attic stuffed in haste."

"Are you setting up a practice here?"

"In a way. Not a law practice. I'm done with that, thank goodness. I came to realize that law is whatever people want it to be. The same for morality."

"Where did you learn that?"

"I had a gulp of it in law school, afterwards I was saturated with too many courtroom chasers. The internet confirms it daily."

"If not law, what is your new practice?"

82

Jerry did not respond. Linda hazarded a guess.

"A minister?"

Jerry nearly choked on his beer.

"No, not a minister. I've taken up writing, which now that you brought it up might be close to a minister. Darn, I wish that you hadn't made that connection."

"Sorry."

Jerry continued with his thought.

"Law is like divinity, its whatever you choose it to be. You know, there is a frightening similarity between stories in holy books and essays written by college freshmen. I'll try to avoid that going forward. Thanks Linda. This is a good place to listen," he added, looking around at the bar.

Linda nodded her agreement.

"What do you write? Truth or fiction?"

"Is there a difference? Each of us construct a separate realit. I simply write mine down. I'm a literary hermit."

'I see."

"You're too polite to ask. It means I don't publish much."

Linda laughed.

"I've published nothing, so a little is a lot."

"I imagine that I sit here waiting for Godot, wasting time, as he won't leave any of his houses here in town, let alone set foot in this bar. I'm not sure why, as it has passed inspection.

"See," he said, pointing to a government certificate on the wall, proud of someone else's effort. "But Godot's story has already been written. We've come to expect his absence; I doubt that we would recognize him if he did return. Aside from a few stragglers, mankind has moved on."

"This is as good a waiting room as any I've sat in."

"Groundhog Day was set over in Punxatawney," Jerry stated, waving idly in what could have been the correct direction. He said it in such a way that the distant town could have been a sound stage a block away from where they sat.

Linda nodded.

"People universally claim to love the movie. Would they love that life?"

"Would you?"

Linda thought the question rhetorical, but she answered it anyway, truthfully, with a shrug.

"We relive the same day, on screen or off. Maybe the presence of small furry animals keeps it interesting."

"You may be on to something there, Linda. You've confirmed the joy that seriousness has a short half life in bars."

"We don't listen to each other these days. We don't listen to each other's gods. We listen only to ourselves. Enough about that. You are staying in the Dietz house?"

"Yes. Where do you live?"

"On Jefferson."

"In that magnificent home with the pool and tennis court? I notice that the neighbor has an ornate tree house that overlooks the surrounding walls."

"No, I'm across and down the street. The one-story brick ranch, one of more unusual, translated as modern, in the district. It's anti magnificent is how I've heard it described. I do my best to enhance the attractiveness of my neighbors' abodes by keeping mine modest."

"Did you build it?"

"Me?" Jerry chuckled.

"No, I'm not talented that way. The previous structure burned back in the fifties, which was when my house was built. This was before the district was historical. Strange, isn't it?"

"What's strange?"

"I don't know. I lost my train of thought. Life, maybe?"

"Are you married, Jerry?"

"Not at the moment. She was too controlling. Women are either too, or nothing. Goldilocks would have been forever frustrated if she'd been male."

"What are you looking for?"

"I'm moderately affluent. I can afford ten carat love. It's not actual love, but I'm accustomed to disappointment. In brief, I'm looking for nothing."

"Pretend that you are madly in love with me and tell me the truth."

"I'd tell you the truth anyway."

"Too bad. I'm disappointed. Truthfulness is such a worthless quality in a man."

"I think that women rarely believe men. Its simpler to tell the truth."

Linda lifted her glass as if in toast but did not drink. She replaced it on the bar.

"No toast to that? I date from time to time. I could try to squeeze you in Linda, but I can't make any promises. If you want promises stop in at one of the temples."

"I can see why you are in such demand. But I'm confused. What about the faithful part?"

"It has a different connotation."

"Oh. Well let me think about that."

Linda lifted the club soda again, and emptied it, motioning to the bartender for a refill.

"There are a lot of churches. All probably started by men. Only a male could invent such crazy ideas as all these competing, omnipotent gods, and then blame women for the subsequent disasters."

Yellowstone brought the glass of beer to his lips in agreement.

"At least some of us have transitioned to believing in sports. I see these new faith symbols in the rear windows of cars, 13.1, 26.2."

"I thought that those were some scriptural reference."

"They are, just of a new obsession. At least in sports one doesn't have to wait thousands of years to be disappointed. And one can have a beer during the service."

"Why do they call you Yellowstone?"

Jerry pulled his keys from his jacket pocket. Dangling from one end, encased in some sort of bezel was a large coin.

"It's a 1999 silver dollar, with Old Faithful on one side and a buffalo on the reverse. From Yellowstone."

Jerry set the keys on the bar and then removed his glasses and set them beside the keys.

"I can see better without these. I broke my new glasses, and these are from years ago. I'm usually much more fashionable Linda. The prescription is so out of date that with them I can only see yesterday. Hey, I could loan you these when my new ones are repaired. I've heard that you enjoy the past."

To Linda's look of surprise, Jerry responded, "Brentville is a small town."

"Let me see your spectacles."

He handed them to her, and she tried them on, saying, "These are very old. Are you a closet hoarder?"

Jerry shrugged.

"I can't see as far as the door, let alone as far as yesterday. They won't help me."

She smiled and set them back on the bar.

"You are a hoarder, I can tell."

"Because you are one yourself?"

"I like to think that I'm cured.   What about you? What else do you have squirreled away?"

"That I'm willing to admit? Oh, lots of things. You never know what may end up in a museum one day. We hoarders are preservationists."

"You're just not as organized as an historical society, is that the big difference?"

"That's as good a description as any. I haven't heard of a cure. You're healthy now?"

Linda started, unsure of the nature of the question.

"I used to be a hoarder Jerry, when I lived in my own yesterday. Now I rent in the past of vacant strangers. Believe me, there is none of my clutter to be found there."

"Are you another gold hunter?"

"A gold hunter?" Linda echoed as response, her voice concerned.

"Detectors. Gold hunters must have learned American history from Hollywood University, with a major in National Treasure. I'm surprised they don't have their own church in town. That's an idea.

Yellowstone pulled a small notebook and a pen from his shirt pocket and scribbled a note and then replaced them like a gun to its holster.

"Reality is whatever the three pounds locked behind two small, blue tinted windows decides it to be. Is it any wonder that these gold bugs see Nicolas Cage as the narrator of a documentary? They envision storerooms and vaults of gold. There is no gold in the state. But still they come. Like you?"

"What do you mean? Linda was still perplexed. "A gold digger? At my age? As far as I know this area doesn't have much in inventory when it comes to sugar daddies. And those that do exist aren't looking for me. Thanks for the compliment."

Linda was unable to let the subject drop.

"Me, a gold digger? Maybe 40, or 30 years ago, alright," she conceded in response to the raised eyebrows of her interlocuter. "Forty years."

"I might have considered it at one point in my life, but really, it seems to involve a great deal of work. There is a reason that rich men are still available to be chased."

"Excuse me for interrupting your alternative past life, but I am talking about actual gold."

Linda felt her stomach tighten, but she said nothing.

"You must know. Gold coins, bars, that sort of thing. Civil war intrigue and ambushed confederate or union gold shipments."

"Sorry, Jerry. No, I am not searching for gold. I'm weary, like you. How much ambition does one person need? Or for that matter, how much gold?"

"Ambition can be healthy.'

"Even in a woman?"

"Touché."

"When people, notice I didn't say me, when people say that a man, or a woman has ambition, they want that person to have a certain type of ambition. Like the godless are required to submit not simply to religion, but a certain flavor.

At this point in my life, no ambition is seen as a virtue, not a sin. Survival is sufficient ambition. I had friends who had been overstuffed with ambition, but little else."

"I find that surprising. That you had friends. You strike me as being too strong."

"Strength can be a weakness. Success can be Midas' touch."

"So says the woman who brought gold to the temple of lost gold."

"What does that mean?"

"I'm not sure. I thought it sounded clever."

"You didn't write it down."

Jerry drank from his nearly empty glass of beer.

"Why the mystery?"

"Which mystery?"

"About your past. Pretend that I am writing your biography. It's research."

"There is nothing to tell."

"I don't believe that. You're hoarding. See, you are still sick."

Linda did not jump this time at his unintended double entendre.

"I'm, oh how did you term it? I'm preserving. But our pasts do have one item in common. I wore glasses in the past also, just like you."

"That's two, not one. What is your link to Brentville, I wonder. You could have been married a half dozen times; your maiden name washed so often that you'd be hard pressed to recognize it yourself."

"Tell me more about my past. Pretend that I have amnesia or that I'm a character in one of your books. Do you write plays? I could be, oh, not the leading lady, but a villain. You'd need a theater group."

"You are already."

"I am?"

"Absolutely. Except that it's not my play, all of Brentville is writing and rewriting it."

"Y'all are assigning me a larger role than I deserve."

"We're bored," Jerry said half jokingly.

Linda put on a fake pout.

"What is the verdict?"

"It ranges from eccentric to witness protection."

"Can I be both?"

"I suppose so. You tell me Linda; you have final control over the character. Which is it?"

"I should dream a lie that you'll believe."

"I believe you."

"You do?"

"I used to believe no one. Now, I believe everyone, it's easier on the brain than skepticism. Tell the truth and believe everything. It works out well most of the time."

"And when it doesn't?"

"You come home to Brentville."

Linda was not sure if he was serious or not.

"It's a small planet, and I've managed to shrink it. I've bled away the billions of tweets and dweebs and ads that inflated it. He spread his arms as if to encompass the entirety of this concentrated, improved world.

"The universe is between our ears," withdrawing his arms to touch his own.

"When I was twelve, a favorite uncle of mine told me to enjoy it, because after that year it would be all downhill.

I had no idea what he meant at the time. Ninety percent of life's fun is consumed by the time a boy becomes a teenager, and you limp along for the subsequent decades parsimoniously gnawing the precious little that remains. I think that Bar Mitzvah translates to 'it's over chump'."

"I doubt that," Linda said with a smile.

When Linda had arrived, only Jerry and the couple at a nearby table had been present along with the bartender.

Now, the spot was nearly half full. Despite the hum of bar conversation, Linda noticed that this was the third Pink Floyd song in succession.

Jerry devined her thought.

"It's incredible that their music is sold over the counter, no prescription necessary. Its not really dance music though."

Linda nodded in agreement and took a sip of club soda.

"This is pleasant. Its enough. I've given up on the world beyond the perimeter. I didn't realize how much I missed Brentville until I returned. Still, I can almost convince myself that I can manage to flourish in this small territory.   can be content here."

"As if this is all that exists, all that remains of a world that you no longer own a piece of. Brentville is your island, your garden of Eden?"

"Yes, exactly."

Linda could not help but pass on the sentiment that had been directed at her.

"You should join the town's marketing committee."

"I have. I did that a week after I returned."

Linda was relieved that he did not ask her which committees she had joined.

89

"I haven't enlisted in a church."

"Brentville has so many beautiful ones to choose from."

"Which is yours?"

"I haven't decided yet."

They both let the lie pass.

"Churches are attractive like Venus flytraps, where the victims are not hapless, but overjoyed to provide nourishment over and over again each week like an infatuated lover."

"Is that so bad? Its their choice."

"Good and bad no longer matter, especially not within hallowed walls of this church in which we find ourselves."

"It's our essential quality that counts."

"Free will?" Linda guessed.

"No. That's crap."

"It's rebellious, dissatisfaction, arrogance, curiosity."

"Is that three or four? "

"Its arrogance disguised as disobedience. We've more in common with the devil than we dare admit."

"Eden was ok, but God had to go and ruin it."

"I must have read a different version."

"But I've found it here."

"Eden?"

"Close enough."

Linda recalled the man whose words had brought her back to Brentville.

"I wonder where he is now?" she said aloud.

"Who?"

"Someone I never knew."

Yellowstone regarded Linda warily.

"Is that club soda or vodka?"

"It is that way, I suppose. Strangers impact us more than those close to us. They provide the necessary detours in our lives. They don't care about us and that helps immensely."

"To strangers?" Yellowstone proposed.

They drank together.

"Too late I learned that not only can't you can't have it all, but all is not enough".

"Its refreshing to see people talking to each other face to face and not on their phones. People are immersed in these devious, all demanding electronics. Worse, they are not wireless, they require feeding more frequently than a newborn, with no possibility of future love."

"They have an app to monitor your addiction."

Linda looked at Yellowstone and sighed.

"Do they turn off the electronics in here? They do that in certain pubs in London."

"Bully for them, but this is not London. Our Victorian Christmas notwithstanding. Which reminds me."

Zeke spotted Linda and his former law partner sitting at the bar, their backs towards the entrance, awaiting his arrival. As he reached the pair, the first words he heard surprised him.

"It's a little early, and we hardly know each other."

"You don't know Linda at all, Jerry," Zeke interjected, concerned where this conversation had been going.

"Neither do you, Zeke," Jerry replied, his attorney's skill still sharp. "That means we are even," he added, returning his attention to Linda.

"Would you like to attend the dance with me?"

"What dance?" Linda and Zeke asked simultaneously.

"I'm asking Linda, Zeke," Jerry answered smugly.

Linda wondered if the two former attorneys had rehearsed this scene and dialogue.

"No," she decided, "this was genuine."

If she had thought otherwise, she'd have walked out. "No, you wouldn't," her inner voice admonished.

"The Christmas dance?" Zeke asked, continuing his questioning.

"As in December Christmas? Not Christmas in July?" Linda added.

"December Christmas, that's the one I'm asking about."

"That is six months away, Jerry," Linda noted. She paused, looking from one man to the other, then completed her thought.

"I might be taken by then," she said flatly, her tone disconcerting the two experienced lawyers. The men glanced at each quizzically.

Linda's mind raced. This town was too insular to sustain long term lies.

"What about our," her inner voice started to ask.

"It's a brief lie, a half truth, more than half as we are in a bar," she waffled to the voice.

"You lie better than you did a week ago," the interior voice said before falling silent.

Jerry was the first to regain his composure.

"If you are taken by then, I will bow out. Graciously."

"Why such a long advance notice?" Linda asked. "Do you need time to take lessons?" she laughed.

"As a matter of fact, I do," Jerry replied, letting Linda squirm before jointing her in laughter. "Six months should be just about enough time, don't you agree?"

"I imagine that you're an accomplished dancer yourself, Linda," Zeke said, not wanting to be overlooked in the this verbal tango.

"You could start a dance club in Brentville."

"There isn't one?"

"No. I'll have to drive to..."

"You need something to do," Zeke interrupted. "You might be able to use the old opera house, I have a connection."

"I'll consider it," Linda said, her second lie in as many minutes. She would do nothing of the kind and poor Jerry would have to drive to wherever.

The unasked question remained unanswered

Will you still be here at Christmas?

Linda had no answer to it, not in any of the ways it could have been intended.

She would not be at the dance, she would either be already taken or near enough that she would be in no condition to dance.

Besides her own failing health, she had no desire to change anything about this, her final layover. She would not risk injuring this delicate town. She could look but not touch.

"I'd love to go with you," she said with a wide smile. That makes three lies, she said to herself. Ho, ho, ho.

"Promise?"

"I'll try. I don't know you well enough to make you a promise, and not nearly well enough to keep it if I did."

Zeke was not pleased but Christmas was many months away.

"Has Jerry shown you his fetish yet?"

"We haven't progessed that rapidly," Linda replied coyly, a bit confused.

"Its there on the bar."

"Oh, the coin from Yelllowstone. Yes, I've seen it."

"He says it was made especially for him, regular blasts and the stamina of a bull. He's dead on about the bull part."

Jerry blushed.

"And he is new in town, about two years."

"I see that we do have things in common," Linda joked.

"His friends call him Yellowstone. I've known him too long, so I call him Jerry."

"Two years is a long time?"

"I've known him since childhood. But he moved away for a while, but now he is back. To the promised land."

Zeke and Yellowstone exchanged a quick glance, one that Linda took to be a negotiation, the bargain completed wordlessly in a few seconds. She did not like it , but like many things she disliked, she ignored it.

"And before 1999 Jerry?"

"What do you mean?"

"This coin was minted in 1999?"

"So?"

"Well, what did you carry before 1999?"

He said nothing, leaving time for Zeke to chime in, "If I remember correctly, it was a clad dime, small and a bit brassy."

"Zeke likes to talk."

There was an awkward silence, that melted when Jerry added, "So do I."

"I was such an honest child, and that made me quiet," he told them with the seriousness of a first beer.

"He's outgrown it."

"When did that happen?"

"I can't provide an exact date, but it has been a while. Once I learned that telling the truth and politeness were guidelines and not actual constraints, I became much more vocal."

"You've described the ideal attorney."

"Thank you."

"If you don't remember when, do you remember how?"

"It must have been the sheer volume of gossip, false rumor and well directed insult that finally broke down my resistance. It has really made me a happier, more contented person."

"Don't forget verbose."

"Thanks, Zeke."

"You told me earlier that telling the truth is simpler."

"I did indeed. I also said that there was no difference between truth and fiction."

"Did you?"

"Although, truth be told, or in this case truth be considered, I generally settle for interesting, like the for-profit media does. Anyway, Linda, interesting is my go-to ingredient. If it tastes interesting, people will swallow any empty calories, including".

"Poison?"

"See, you understand. It's like this discussion that we are having, it's bar talk, we agree to certain unspoken rules. Even if the man has one beer and the woman a club soda."

"And? "

"And the whole country is a bar. Churches criticize taverns because they fear the competition. Each offers temporary hope. Some supercilious fools simply don't see the truth of this. Like that Mike Hayes."

"What about him? He is a god-fearing man."

"He is a fearful man, period. He goes to churches every day."

"Churches?"

"Whichever ones are open, whatever they offer. If God wants to reach me, He can. Easily. This is a tiny planet."

Jerry winked.

"Maybe an idea for a new book."

Jerry finished his one beer, now warm and slid from the barstool.

"The wise go to bars to prove their stupidity, the less gifted to demonstrate their cleverness. But both leave too soon.

Linda, it was indeed a pleasure to meet you. I will keep you abreast of my dance improvement. Zeke, we can talk later. I have to go."

"No stay. Finish your business."

Linda excused herself and slid from the bar stool. She said nothing more but left her keys behind, signaling her return. She stepped in the direcion of the toilet, leaving the men to continue their battle."

"She's bad news, Zeke."

"I'll settle for any news."

"For how long?"

"I can't answer that. Can you?"

His former partner replied with silence, then gathered his own keys and left.

In the ladies' restroom Linda thought for a moment. In another lifetime, men, those worth permitting to pursue her had all been older than she, some much older. When had they become younger? For here in Brentville they were all, without exception, younger than she.

CHAPTER EIGHTEEN

Whether it was part of her explorations or necessitated by lack of transportation, the long, daily walks that Linda took were invigorating.

Both her energy levels and wind had improved.

Maybe she would take up pole vaulting again, she thought briefly before abandoning the whim.

That level of crazy thought brought her back suddenly to reality. If she could conceive of such a wild idea, then whatever poison pooled in her brain remained. Hers would be a healthy corpse, from the neck down she would be in the best condition in years, but still dead. It was not the most compelling of testimonials from the small, but comprehensive YMCA that she had joined.

She thought that science would benefit from a final donation of her body, but no, she wanted to travel no more, alive or dead.

She smiled, not for the first time, thinking of her secret. It was not the content of the secret that pleased her, how could it, but that she had a secree. In the quiet of the restaurant, she heard the ticking of the clock. The arrival of more diners would obscure its sound, but it's hands would still advance at the same, consistent pace. Whether it was a sprint or sitting quietly with only a cup of tea as companion, tick, tick, tick the clock droned.

At a far table, a young woman sat, immersed in her solitary cell. The white earbuds that she wore provided immunity from unwanted advances. She could wave off a persistent hopeful without giving offense as if the electronic devices were a diplomatic passport.

Those little white dots permitted poorish, boorish behavior, made of each wearer an eccentric among eccentrics.

Linda suspected that the woman displayed them deliberately, their presence accentuated her blond hair. They were both a lure and a deterrent, and she likely enjoyed experiencing their impact.

"Would she regret her aloofness when her blond hair was streaked with gray like mine?" Linda wondered.

This small, pocketable device, designed to aid communication, served to deter it, to transform existence into a constant, meaningless quiz sh iw without winners, only contestants.

The clock continued its ticking. Linda pretended that she was like every other living thing, that sound could be ignored, it's regularity eternal. Death was agreeably distant, for the others, like the woman with her earbuds, not due later this year, like snow and cold and darkness.

The current joy was that today extended before that finality. Today could last forever, it's potential so immense, powerful to push the year's end, her end, not into a bleak future, but into a region beyond that. She could hop into the past.

The future was endless winter, the past forever summer.

The tea before her would grow tepid, the clouds of cream would slow and then halt their swirling and coalesce into a liquid offering permanence, and when it was gone, when she had consumed its properties of sedative and stimulant, she would order another. Perhaps the clock would cease its monotonous mockery.

She felt herself a mayfly, cramming a lifetime into a bag too small.

Tea, it was a simple activity, readily prolonged and repeated, an anitode to fear.

97

Linda's revelry was disrupted by the arrival of another customer, a family in fact. The girl breezed by, the wake of her sudden passage generating ripples on Linda's cooling beverage. She was followed by her parents, a couple who should have bypassed the restaurant and continued to the YMCA.

"Why do twenty-first century Americans sway? Do they imagine themselves aboard a poorly designed cruise ship?" Linda asked herself.

Soon the restaurant was full, her second cup of tea drunk, the passage of time unheard over the sound of voices. They had their lives. A middle aged man sporting a head scarf was discussing events from his high school, the number 1965 was mentioned several times.

They mentioned the McCabe building and the ongoing discussions to renovate itss opera house, hidden away like the searched for gold. Linda overheard them mention the Cadillac muesum and the illness of ones of its restorers.

"He won't recover," the woman said.

"They could be talking about me," Linda told herself.

Once, a griever she had met in this very café had asked Linda to accompany her to the funeral home for visitation. The request had been delivered with such emotion, that Linda had accepted, reluctantly. It had been a dreadful mistake.

Death was now so close that Linda should have stayed as far away from its domain as possible.

No rendezvous, not yet. The unpleasant meeting with Death would occur too soon. Linda decided that she wanted no visitation for herself. Let any mourners grieve from afar.

The trip to the parlor had become immeasurably worse when she gazed upon the face of the unknown woman deceased in the casket. It could have been her own mother. Linda nearly fainted. She clutched onto the left arm of the stranger who had asked her to attend. It was a reversal of support, lost on the stranger. Either she had suffered a similar jolt of emotion, or she was too shaken to notice Linda's reaction.

Linda forced herself to regard the corpse again. It had been decades since the burial of her own mother, the memory of her mother was fading, the image vague. Maybe it was just the age of the woman, no, there was no doubt. The deceased could have been mother.

Linda felt her companion shift slightly, she was ready to move along. They did so, separated when the woman whispered, "Thank you." Linda moved away, unsteady on her feet. She walked stiffly, in small steps, to the restroom where she forced herself again to gaze, this time in the mirror, fearful of seeing her mother's face there, relieved when the door opened, and another stranger entered. Linda looked quickly into the glass, seeing only her own image. She felt her heart restart, the sound of flowing blood filled her ears, and her chest heaved with might have been her first breath. The combination of stress and its sudden lifting created a state of nonmind, where she teetered between overwhelming concern and near unconsciousness. It surrounded her with a transparent numbness, the unthinking courage of the exhausted.

"Never again," she said to the familiar reflection.

Linda sipped the now cool tea. She had the perfect life in Brentville, that of a semi- nomad. She had acquaintances here, not sure if any were friends. Friends were people while road acquaintances weren't, she did not worry about disappointing them.

Outside on the sidewalk, the café's proprietor and her husband were meeting with a carpenter tasked with redoing the entrance. The woman chose the color scheme, leaving the men to finalize details within the constraints that she had firmly set.

The town was peaceful, most of the crime of future occurring on its northern side. It hosted a horde of ever changing futurists, ready to descend into the valley and destroy it. It represented what Linda had once been. She sometimes felt herself blessed as an extra in a Hallmark movie, one with a sophisticated script and elegant set, and one in which she had no dialogue. She was pleased to be out of sight, invisible to nearly one and all. Cream rises to the top, but gold descends to the valley floor.

And while not gold, the café was appointed with brass and ivory lamps, black and white still lifes, it was a play in perpetual dress rehearsal, no audience needed, as the cast was pleased to perform for itself.

Was she up to auditioning, or was she satisfied to be just another extra, a potted plant?

The size and outline of the village was manageable, perfect in its proportions and lack of pretentiousness. It was quaint without being a caricature, genuine and livable. Perfect conditions for a potted plant.

The café was busy, and Linda ordered an omelette as a means of retaining her place. At the next table Linda overheard one stranger telling another

"He had family here, otherwise he'd have been dumped in a hole up in Whitland."

"That's cruel, Jake. And crude."

"I'm going to have that carved on my tombstone, Annie. It's true. They just toss people into holes up there."

"They do not. Whitland is as civilized as Brentville."

"Maybe more so, now that I think about it."

"I wouldn't say that."

Linda knew of Whitland only by secondhand stories, several by Zeke and one that she had read, in of all places, a psychology magazine that she picked up in the local library.

Whitland was a quaint county seat, dependent on the local petroleum industry. It was surrounded by bucolic rolling hills, and lay an hour's ride northwest, on the far side of the Allegheny National Forest.

It was an American cousin of an English village, prideful of past glories, insular, confident of survival, hopeful for prosperity.

An hour's ride through the forest to a picturesque town. It was to Linda a nightmare, too horrible to contemplate. It was a Grimm's fairy tale with internal combustion.

The article that she had read described in detail the vast mental hospital, closed for over a decade, that had once been another major source of Whitland's revenue.

Linda pictured the inhabitants. Stuck behind guards while able to enjoy views that extended to whatever reality they constructed for themselves, while on the upper walls of the buildings of the medical complex, a nameless bureaucrat had had installed in stone, the images of the faces of numerous Greek gods. Surely it counteracted the danger of cure.

A pristine river and a contributary stream flowed through town, past the refinery and numerous operational oil wells that sat on vacated industrial properties. The petroleum was essential to the town's continued existence.

"They aren't as civilized as we are Jake. They live beyond the forest," the woman was saying.

"We're wonderful neighbors, but the miles and miles of trees make for an equally wonderful fence.

"Someone who understands the value of isolation," Linda reflected. "Maybe the trees were her own totems. If so did that make her equally mentally ill? Walls, everyone needs them, as much as they need a roof, for protection. And Zeke, what was his role, a guard?"

She finished the tea and decided to extend the lazy day by next treating herself to an early dessert.

Dil's was decorated with 1950s or 1960s lime green blenders, mismatched wooden tables paired with spindly chairs. Black raspberry ice cream, a delicacy of that region of the state, was the seasonal flavor.

"Great minds think alike," the familiar voice said.

She looked up into the eyes of Zeke, who soon joined her with his own cone of black raspberry sweetness.

"What did you know about Whitland?"

"Its ok, a nice enough town if you ignore the refinery. It's the other side of the forest. The forest defines us somewhat, in case you haven't noticed. It intervenes like an older brother, or an uncle. The ride through 500,000 acres is worth it, with a few stops in between."

"It sounds wonderful," she said after Zeke had finished.

"When can we go?"

"Seriously?"

"You've transformed this distant here be dragons land into a virtual paradise."

"Well, Linda, would the day after tomorrow be too soon. I'm afraid that I may have oversold Whitland. He wanted to lower expectations, while he himself was overjoyed at this new found enthusiasm."

"Sorry, I truly am," Linda said.

"I was joking. It was a poor topic for humor, I see that now."

"No problem."

"You know that I don't travel beyond,"

"These conifer confines," he finished for her.

"I have my own Eden here, and so far I have not glimpsed one serpent."

"Only a few attorneys," he said, attempting his own joke.

CHAPTER NINETEEN

Having suggested that Hannah stop by after her shift at GE so that they could walk together to the diner, Linda had left the front door ajar.

Hannah arrived on time; a backpack strapped over her shoulders like the high school student she remained and ascended the long staircase to change clothes in an upstairs room.

Hannah descended the staircase a few minutes later, wearing shorts, a T shirt, and sneakers, instead of her waitress' uniform.

"I swapped shifts, so we could have more time to talk," Hannah explained.

"Perfect," was all that Linda said, amazed at how at ease she was with this stranger, young enough to be her granddaughter.

As they made their way to the front door, Hannah hesitated, intrigued by the title of a book that lay open on a nearby coffee table. Hannah lifted it and glanced at the text before closing the book again, keeping her right forefinger inside to save Linda's spot. She looked again at the title, then replaced the book as she had found it."

"No Exit, it could have been written for me."

"I picked it up at the Shed," Linda informed Hannah, referring to the bookstore on Main.

"Its in English as well as the original French."

Hannah retrieved the book again. The book indeed was bilingual, with only the left side pages in English.

"French? Here in Brentville? Why?" Hannah scoffed.

"Why not?"

Hannah glanced again at the cover.

"Jean Paul Sartre. Not local, I suppose?"

"No, French."

Linda continued.

"It's a play set in Hell, with three characters, locked together forever. Attacking and arguing with each other."

Hannah snorted in amusement.

"I was wrong. It's totally appropriate for this town. It is not surprising that you found it in the district. So Brentville is Hell? Finally, someone who understands."

Linda laughed.

"I would not put it quite that way. Strangely, the movie Groundhog Day and No Exit have the same premise, with the outcome altered by cast size. Sartre's vision worked because there were only three characters. "

Hannah snorted again.

"It took a foreigner to notice that Brentville is Hell. We are so blind."

"With three thousand characters the play now set in Brentville, transforms into Heaven. The caterpillar morphs into a butterfly."

Hannah laughed uproariously, the simplest riposte to an argument.

"Brentville is Heaven? You obviously aren't French. You should construct another church, Linda. The dozen or that already exist don't satisfy you."

"That is an excellent idea. We can begin our walk with a challenge. Let's walk by several and inspect them along the route. Perhaps one will fit, but I doubt it."

The two women left the house.

To Linda's delight, the walk was more of a stroll. Hannah's deadline no longer constituted a worry.

They departed from the address on Snowden, ambled along White, crossed Bankfield Creek and then Main Street. Their steps carried them along the west side of a magnificent church, constructed in red stone. They paused before the home of its newly appointed minister. It was a beautiful presbytery, in the style of a French second empire manse.

"If this is the reward for a new church founder, then maybe I will start a No Exit branch," Linda joked.

The women's progress slowed as the road ascended, and they halted to rest for several minutes in front of the Rebecca Arthurs memorial library.

"It reminds me of a post office."

"It does? I don't see it."

"Not in style, but in function. Printed stories pass from one stranger to another, and letters travel from one friend to another. The same, whether books or mail."

"Emily says that you don't get much mail."

"I get too much."

"I used to so like the scent of paper and glue and ink, both in post offices and libraries," the older woman reminisced.

A thought came to Linda.

"What about you? Your mailbox must be stuffed with letters and instructions from universities. Are you going to college in the fall? I'm being nosy. Sorry," she said with a smile.

What are your plans, Hannah?"

"For today? Or for my future?"

"Future," Linda answered in a near whisper, the word sounding strange to her own ears.

"I've been accepted by a local college."

Linda pictured herself as Hannah, her joy at being able to attend a local college in this semi-rural setting. It would be a small, quiet scholarly campus, tucked away where one could hear others and oneself think.

Hannah's vague response that she had been accepted at such a school pleased Linda immensely.

Smiles came to their faces, while Hannah told herself, "I have no intention of attending this or any other regular college. Why delay my life any longer? It was good for appearances, and it was plan F, if all other plans failed."

Hannah envisioned excitement, her preferred institute of advanced education the university of the world, her freshman year at the campus of America. And for the second year? The world was big, by comparison, Brentville was nothing more than a simple community college.

"Don't you miss your life? Whatever your life was before you ended up here? I don't mean to be nosy, but it is my turn."

"This is my life. I didn't end up here by accident. Brentville was a deliberate choice."

Traffic noise increased as they neared the freeway. Conversation became difficult, the smell of exhaust assaulted Linda's nose. It reeked of the future, the odor as nauseating as the toilets in the gardens of Versailles.

The pair scurried beneath the freeway and turned east on Cemetery Road, resuming their ramble, crossing in front of the school track where Linda had first seen Hannah. And Emily. And Zeke.

So long ago, that first encounter. How many days? Better not to count, but Linda could not banish the sight of a hourglass with its diminishing quantity of sand.

Hannah, and Emily, and Zeke. "Who are they?" she asked herself. Friends was the word that she landed on. Mike too was a friend, after a fashion. "Friends, her escorts in the past," she decided.

The cemetery was well kept, Linda has expected no less. It had but a single drivable loop that provided easy ingress and egress to those bringing the others who would remain.

Without exception, the monuments were carved with names and years. She recognized some of the names as being similarly engraved on downtown buildings.

Linda observed the specially designed flags that sat low next to numerous markers; they indicated the bunks of sleeping firefighters.

They passed one stone of a Civil War veteran, 1843-1914 Baltimore artillery, CSA.

"What was his story?" Linda wondered about the man buried far from home.

As the women approached Linda's own assigned place of repose, Linda did not slow, instead she increased their pace. The lot had been expensive per square foot, but a bargain when calculated per overnight stay.

Linda did not stop before her vacant rectangle, nor did she indicate to Hannah that this would be her address when the lease expired on Snowden. There was no need to rehearse a brief play that would open and close the same afternoon, what without doubt would be a poorly attended matinee performance of a farce. She hoped only that it would not rain that day.

Linda's abrupt laughter at her private macabre future remembrance startled Hannah, who appeared lost in her own personal reflection.

They looked at each other, the scene awkward and disconcerting. Neither said anything, neither sure as to what had just occurred. A moment later, the women moved on.

As Linda's graveside fell further behind them, Linda slowed her step.

"Shall we sit?" Hannah asked. Linda appeared fatigued, sick perhaps.

"Are you ok, Linda?"

"Yes, I'm fine. I'm just a bit nostalgic."

"Nostalgia should make you happy."

"You would think so. Maybe its too much happiness," she said in an attempt to allay Hannah's concern.

"Its like too much gorgeous sunlight causes sunstroke. Really, I am ok. I prefer to stand."

"So would they," Hannah said, glancing around.

As out of the blue as Linda's laugh had been, Hannah went on with her own odd thought.

"When you do the subtraction of the dates on the marble, the answer is about the same, eighty years or so. Its not long."

"Sometimes, I think it is too long," Linda countered.

"Why do they emphasize the dates on the stones? It's the dash in between that matters."

"That is what the stories told at family reunions accomplish. They fill in that dash for those left behind."

Linda sensed that family reunions were not a frequent occurrence in either of their lives. She stretched and started along the road, Hannah at her side.

"Eighty years, that is a C plus in Life's grading system, where attendance counts more than performance. I remember high school, or I think that what I remember is what actually happened. Is high school still like that?"

"Yes, the same as you remember. Look, Linda," Hannah exclaimed, pointing at a larger, older marker a dozen paces away.

"Ninety eight years. An A."

"I remember boys from high school. And lessons about men. It's funny, we learned men in home economics."

"What's that?"

"Another part of the forgotten past. It was a big part of the class, so important that it was not mentioned in the syllabus."

"It was replaced by sex education? That was a poor trade."

"Yes, but not very effectively. There was no test, that came later, in real life. But I still remember the classification system. Like one remembers the times tables."

"Tell me more. Do you mean like how some men are useful, but they are ultimately unnecessary?"

"I think that were taught the exact opposite. Times change apparently."

Hannah's eighteen years coalesced, and she said, "For men, sex is life, for women life is sex. Men will simply have to wait."

"I classify men. Why not? They categorize me as soon as I walk into the room."

"How do you rate men?"

"Don't you?"

"I suppose so."

"A normal man would be perfect for me."

"Let me know when you find one," Linda replied

"One who isn't a moron or do moronic stuff. One who has a decent career. For you that would be Zeke."

"For me?"

"Sure. He has, had a fantastic career, he has money, he's smart."

"It sounds like he's just perfect for you, smart and rich enough," Linda joked.

"That's the problem, he had a career, he has money but no youth. He's low on youth," Hannah said, and laughed nervously, unsure of Linda's reaction.

Linda only nodded.

"You and Zeke are perfectly matched," Hannah went on. To herself Hannah added, "But you are dying, or so you imply." Why would Linda lie about such a thing? So too bad for Zeke. Hannah really did care for him. He didn't reside entirely in the past. Soon, if she was correct in her assumptions, Linda would be a part of Zeke's past. Zeke had no children, no junior Zeke for her.

"Oh well," Hannah said to Linda, "I have no time for men, rich or poor, smart or moronic. Mary taught me that.

Eve should have kept the apple to herself and left Adam in his pre man-cave, gardening. Like Mike Hayes." Hannah laughed but Linda did not join in.

"Biting the fruit may have been a sin in the eyes of Adam's god, but sharing it was Eve's big mistake." She laughed again.

It was not a pretty laugh for a pretty girl. She would need to work on that, Linda thought for some reason

"I'm not so sure now about Eden, but Brentville is close to Heaven. Not for you but it could be. And it may not be Heaven for me either, not for eternity, but for a lifetime, yours or mine, and a lifetime of Heaven is sufficient."

"My life is nothing," Hannah said, leaving no room for dispute.

"Welcome to the club, so is mine."

"Then my life is less than nothing."

The girl paused, then continued speaking.

"They teach us that life is what you make it."

Linda remained silent.

"But most of us can't make anything at all."

"A life, make a life."

"A life, that is a joke, some of the girls think that making a baby is making a life."

"It can be."

"I want more."

"You want different, not more."

109

"Maybe. So, yes, I want different."

Hannah paused then added, "You still don't understand."

"Oh, but I do. I understand very well. Your song has the same melody as most, only the lyrics are different."

"Which song?"

"The emotions don't change. Your song was my song, but I've switched to a new tune. One that I found myself humming more and more often."

Linda smiled.

"I'd tell you to wait."

"Everyone tells me to wait, like a dog."

"Hannah, I am not telling you to wait."

"But you just..."

"Waiting doesn't work. The wait becomes the focus, the end to be avoided.

No, don't wait. Act! But just a bit. Act, and then think. Its between waiting and acting. Act a bit, then stop and think.

Think of it like entering a swimming pool. You can't wait for it to warm up, because it never does, does it? Or you can cannon ball in, but there is no reversing if the water is frigid or boiling.

Eighty years. You have time.

So think, Hannah, don't wait to act, but don't wait to think either.

Think, act, think, act. Its not that damned difficult.

I've spoken too much. Its not the best advice that I or anyone can offer you, but it's the only good advice that I believe that you will take or consider."

"I'll consider it."

Hannah thought for a moment longer.

"Did it work for you?"

"I can't say that it worked well. I am where I am. I can't redo it."

"You have been attempting to redo it since your arrival."

Linda laughed. "You think that I am trying to redo my life?"

"Aren't you?"

The older woman laughed again. "I can redo nothing."

110

"Act and think?"

"I've used my quota, Hannah. Its funny but now all that I can do is wait."

They were silent for a while, each in their own memories of the past and expectations of the future.

Simultaneously, the two women began to stroll again.

"What else do you remember?"

"About high school?"

Hannah nodded.

"Ambition and boys. It was a tradeoff. I concluded one day that Nature would create more boys, while my ambition was mine alone."

"I know what you mean," Hannah said, nodding her head.

"And then life swept by. In hindsight it strikes me as random, life I mean. There is no plan, only the delusion of one. Innumerable atoms wandering around muttering, "Why me?""

Hannah was correct, Linda thought. She did find comfort in yesterday.

"And you dream of tomorrow?"

"Certainly."

"You are rich in tomorrows."

"Tomorrow frightens you," Hannah stated, the words not a question.

"Tomorrow wearies me. It is exhausting. Fresh and different from one day to the next and knowing that the next following days will be filled with the unforeseen. It's horrible."

"To you. You've described my dream. I bet that it was your dream once."

Linda nodded her assent.

"Each day different, unique. It's dating a new man each evening. So to speak," she added.

"I suppose that it sounds wonderful to you."

Linda was surprised when Hannah shrugged.

"The men that I've dealt with are as clutching as the district. I won't trade a dead anchor for a living one."

Linda smiled. The majority of men she had known had been, if not anchors, then deadweight, best tossed overboard at the first opportunity.

Linda carried a map of the hamlet with her on her strolls. It was not to prevent her becoming lost, for that was impossible, but as a prop when she wanted to stop and observe interesting people and sights. Unfolded, its ungainly precision emitted a permanent certitude.

The women had reached the north easternmost part of Brentville. Linda would venture no further from Snowden.

For the humans passing along, comfortable between its golden lines, the interstate beckoned further travel. Its signs promised as much as any church, all available and affordable just ahead in the kingdom of man. Food, lodging, magnificent sights lay minutes ahead

Here in town, churches stood, labeled A to Z. There were even statues of past and future presidents if your faith ran in that direction.

"I like frozen."

"Frozen what?" Hannah asked, confused.

"Historical Brentville is pretty much frozen and that appeals to me."

"It's a disease, or maybe a glacier. One that spreads. It has tax advantages, and you get to brag about being in the district. You see that, don't you?"

"I guess so. And you don't want to be part of the creeping of the district beyond its current borders."

"Creepy is the word for it. Even if it doesn't reach you by spreading, it pulls you in."

"Is that bad? It's your home after all Hannah."

"I don't want to be an exhibit in my dead great grandmother's world, or worse to be a caretaker of the life of someone long dead."

"There can be a balance. The past is always with us."

"Too much, too much. This past is new to you. It's quaint, isn't it?"

"You said that without screaming."

Hannah responded with a weak smile.

"I'm good at repressing my emotions."

"Since you ask, yes. This past is," Linda said and paused, searching for the correct word.

"Soothing. It has the right Q factor," she finished, her feeble smile echoing that of Hannah.

"I hate that word. I want a world where nothing is quaint, a quaintless, cute-free world. I can't exist in some three-dimensional movie set where there is no second scene."

"So it's Groundhog Day for you."

"No Exit. We are back to where we began."

"Punxsutawney is only 30 miles away."

"I've never been there."

"No?"

"What would be the point?"

"Not all of Brentville is history, Livetown exists. And new people, young people like yourself I mean."

"The newer part is the other side of 80," Hannah said.

"Interstate 80" Linda translated.

"Yes. It's weird, that is where the cemetery is. The dead are in the new town, and you pass your days in the dead district."

Hannah took a breath.

"Does that make sense to you?"

Linda could only shrug. This was too intense a conversation for such a beautiful day. She only had a certain allotment of passion to dispense on a daily basis.

Receiving no answer, Hannah provided the correct response.

"It doesn't make sense to me.

The dead are interred in the future, and we are zombies in the past. I refuse to be buried in Brentville's past, the past that you've embraced. It not your past Linda.

I don't care about the past of the detectors the past of the tourists, you included."

There the girl had said it. To her, Linda was a tourist, a carrier of and a pilgrim to the past.

She wanted to deny it, to claim that she was not a tourist, but she was. It was true, as accurate at that moment as the map that she carried had been when surveyed. She had no right to assign herself another designation.

"You came here to find yesterday. Do you pretend that you arrived in that Twyford four-wheel drive car in the museum? Do you dream that you can force yourself back to that time? Brentville is not a time capsule. There is the new version of your temporal Twyford, gesturing to a passing sedan. It can transport me to my future."

"I could help you with a car, with college. The world is dangerous. The future can be terrible. I appreciate that you want the future.

That amazing new friend at the other end of the internet, the one you found, or who magically reached you, is just as confused as you. They are nothing more than a distant reflection."

"I've heard the stories about these perverts and predators. I'm careful."

"Did you stop to think that it might be you who is the dangerous one?"

Hannah looked at Linda in disbelief.

Was the shock genuine, or was it an innate talent for acting, Linda wondered. Aloud, she said,

"A young woman can be very threatening. Sometimes despite her best intentions."

"A predator might be preferred to a soulmate. Evil doesn't disappoint."

"Are you serious? Mike Hayes told me that you were odd but not creepy," not repeating the entirety of his statement.

"I'll take that as a compliment."

Hannah paused then laughed.

"You and Mike Hayes. That is hilarious! The vegan and the cannibal."

"Where do you get such an idea?" Linda asked, curious about the repeated vegan references.

"People talk. I observe. We aren't overflowing with activities in Brentville, in case you haven't noticed. Gossip is free."

Linda was reminded of what a taxi driver in Malta had once told her; the local pastimes were soccer and jealousy.

"Did he tell you about the crazy girlfriend? That is the question on the minds of the bored, me, I don't really care. Not much, but I get bored too. This girlfriend, did she exist outside of his mind? If she did, what was her side of the story? If the woman had been important to the man, well, there had to be some give and take in a relationship, didn't there? A brittle man is as useless as a noodle."

"You are observant."

"I've had to be observant. People talk; people lie. When you listen to a radio, you have no idea what the speaker is actually doing."

"What the hell do I know," Hannah asked in an exhausted voice.

"My parents provided no roadmap except to a salvage yard."

"Where is your father"'

"He is around here somewhere," Hannah replied, as if Linda had asked for the dustpan. Perhaps she had.

"And your mother?"

"Now that I'm older,"

"Yes. Eighteen now," Linda nearly said aloud.

"I think that she must have been a bit like me."

"Oh?"

"In wanting to get away. In wanting to have a future, a good future. But she couldn't resist the men. From what I heard from Gram, she made a play for every third man that passed through. She was an athlete in her own right, you might say. She was a regular toll collector."

"18 years old," Linda reminded herself.

"And this was twenty years before there was even talk of making the interstate other than a free ride."

"Your father, does he live in town?"

"Probably. But I think that any one of three men over 40 could be my dad. The so-called official father, I'm convinced was the result of a coin toss."

"Six months ago, this girl could not legally drive alone after midnight," Linda told herself.

"We have a long tradition of not being a close family. Not living near each other causes that."

"Are you sure that it's not the other way round."

"Maybe. The results are the same."

"It's a dangerous world for a young woman Hannah. The world is not your friend. It is not your oyster, but a jellyfish."

"This is a boring world, a museum made safe under layers of dust. A moment later Hannah disclosed a secret

"I have a plan."

"That makes her dangerous," Linda told herself.

Instead of speaking her mind, Linda smiled, and said, "Well, that's good," in a nonjudgmental tone.

"I don't want to be like you. I don't want to be you."

"You want to be yourself. We all want to be ourselves."

"If that were true people would be so different than they are. Would you be here?"

"It doesn't matter."

"I want my life. I listen to you and Mary and"

"Who is this Mary?"

"Mary Parks, Emily's older sister."

"I see. And you want to follow us?"

"No, no, no. I go the opposite direction. You two are lost in this tiny village. But you can't."

"Is that a question or your verdict?"

"You fit in well with the rest of Brentville. You aren't willing to let me live my life as I please."

"Don't be ridiculous."

It was the wrong approach, Linda realized before the words crossed the short distance separating them.

"I am simply...Hannah, I'm trying to help."

"Oh, I am familiar with that phrase. I've been fed that for months now. Your recipe doesn't taste better than any of the others."

"You're right."

"What?"

"You are 100 percent correct. In everything that you say. And think. And yes, in what you feel. And imagine. Who am I to argue?"

There was silence, with the drone of passing traffic the only sound. Even the birds seemed to be eavesdropping.

"Let's head back. We can listen to the trees, since we can't listen to each other. I don't care about my future, it's as obscure as the fog was this morning. But it's lifted now, for you that is. You can see where you want to go, where you need to step. I'm content to stay in the mist. I want to help Hannah, if I

116

can. I can't obtain a time machine for you, Twyford or other brand, but I could help you with a used car."

"As to the rest of it, it was presumptuous of me to offer advice on yours. Lesson learned, Hannah. I care about, ironically enough to no longer care. Does that make sense?"

"I guess so."

"Great. I realize that I care more about myself, much, much more than any other person. We have that strength in common."

"I guess so," Hannah repeated, and this time she smiled.

"Thanks," she added.

"Don't mention it. I won't," Linda added, and she too smiled, in order to ease what she nevertheless felt had been harsh words. The sentiments behind her latest words would not have been true fifteen minutes previously. They were now.

Hannah was as flawed as Linda had been at the same age. She had vaulted to a greater height than Linda had thought possible for a female. The fall would be proportionally more painful.

The two women stood facing each other at the northern border of Linda's isolation, an unmarked spot on the map where her desires and those of Hannah's diverged.

"I've enjoyed this walk, and our talk Hannah, I do...".

But no words came. They would have been repetitive, the offer already rejected and then withdrawn.

"Bye for now."

Hannah turned west and Linda faced south. Several minutes later, they were separated, but still somehow connected.

During her walk back to Snowden, Linda would listen to the wisdom of trees, and to the gossip of birds, and to the opinion of the wind, and Linda would be content.

"Hannah has my past, and I her future."

CHAPTER TWENTY

Linda woke, determined to visit the cemetery, not as a tourist, not as a prospective resident, but as a mourner, in spirit if not in fact.

She had been a voyeur, a vampire, a student at so many viewings that a trip to the burial grounds would be a form of penance if not a moment of remorse.

She wore her own, recently acquired casket ready dress. It had not made the move with her. Regardless, it now held pride of place in her meagerly hung closet. It was a macabre variant of her long-ago wedding gown.

The black dress fit well, if a bit loosely compared to when she had first tried it on a few months previously. A year ago, she'd have congratulated herself on the weight drop, daily walks and manual labor had rendered her already lithe body tauter. She'd have celebrated with a glass or two of wine. But not today. Her body was following her brain into decline, and while wine could also numb pain, there was none to repress. Pain? No. But there was fear and alcohol would magnify it first before it blocked it out temporarily.

None of her doctors had been willing to give her a year. Persistent, she had consulted the mirror in the master bedroom of her previous home and been sentenced to twelve months.

Was it a sentence or a promise? Another unimportant question. Either answer would suffice

One year, no leap year to extend it, she had noticed on the small, one page calendar

What was it like there, on the other side? Was there an other side? Her questions were silly. They weren't unanswerable, but too readily answered. There were too many answers, but she craved only one.

Her mind captured every detail of the ceremony, and she studied every movement, realizing that her own debut would require nothing more than her presence, and that too would be arranged by a surrogate.

Eulogies are best delivered only slightly rehearsed. It's equally important to both break down and to remember to mention the good bits of a person's life. It's like a secondhand version of America's Got Talent.

Were graveside services the original theater, Linda wondered, the home of the dead serving ironically as the birthing ground of actors.

So much passion and emotion compressed into a single performance. A brief performance.

Oh yes, brief. Eulogies had to be brief, as nothing highlighted the brevity of life as a funeral. In her purse she carried a pair of sensible shoes, a fashion faux pas but her feet would have approved if she had not been able to hitch a ride with one of the genuine mourners.

Sybil was one of the authentic bereaved. After the service, she walked slowly towards Linda, covering the short distance at her own pace.

"I'm pleased to finally meet you. I'm Sybil Cochran."

"The pleasure is mine. I'm Linda Smith."

"I've seen you on your daily walks, but as you can see, I'm in no condition to catch you as you pass by. Did you know James?"

"Ah, no," Linda began but she could think of no plausible reason for being at his funeral. She elected to go with what came to mind.

"It just felt right."

Sybil regarded her with an intensity reminiscent of the US marshal who had once been her neighbor decades ago. Linda remembered his unblinking gaze, his close stance whenever they discussed anything in the driveway between their two yards.

"Oh?" Sybil asked, in a manner that was at once curious and threatening.

A near lie came into Linda's head.

"I walk here so often and I've never...I felt that I owed some sort of dues."

"Dues to the dead, that is quite noble. What of dues for the living?"

Linda treated the statement as rhetorical.

"You must like to walk."

Linda merely nodded.

"I've lost the habit, and unfortunately the ability. Its for the best, as I'm so busy."

The last word was said in such a way that 'in control' could have readily substituted. Linda left the words pass over her as if unheard. One had the right to remain deaf as well as silent.

"You walks must be healthy my dear."

"My dear?" Linda thought. "This woman could be an older sister, much older yes, but".

"They give you something to do."

"Yes, they do. I see that the family is leaving."

Linda stooped down and began to change her shoes.

Sybil stood there, aghast.

Linda's smile was directed earthward as she continued to swap footwear. She had never managed to bring that expression to the face of the marshal.

Shoes exchanged, Linda returned to an upright position and stretched out her right arm.

The two women shook hands, then parted. Linda swung her arms slightly and splayed the fingers of both hands as she walked toward the cemetery driveway. There was a breeze, and it flowed between the digits, cleansing them.

CHAPTER TWENTY-ONE

Jerry and Zeke stood on the wraparound porch of the home of Randy Prentice, hesitant to enter the house. They knew that Randy would not be the same that they had known since childhood. He has introduced them to the old machines that he kept in the barn next to his house, one block south of Main Street. The nineteenth century equipment was obsolete and archaic. He had hauled if from who knows where, abandoned in the woods he had told them, to his workshop, where he tinkered, and repaired and reconditioned the old industrial engines and pumps to a point that they were better than new. For Zeke and Jerry, it had been a relief from constant studies. Although both had gone on to the law, where the only machines were located in offices, they had remained in close touch.

The machines were now on permanent loan to the Cool Springs museum, where Randy had been a fixture. The barn stood empty, its only occupants a few groundhogs and crows.

Randy had kept his hand busy working part time at the Brentville Cadillac museum, but that too had ended shortly before his stroke. His body was now obsolete and archaic, impossible to restore.

Zeke looked up and down the street, hoping to spot someone, anyone, who would provide a delay from this unpleasant task. Instead, he noticed a blue Ford, parked in front and nearly obscured by a white van. He nudged Jerry and nodded in the direction of the Ford.

"That is Sybil Cochran's car."
"Mrs. Cochran? Our old high school teacher?"
"The one and same."
"I thought that she died years ago."

"She is too polite for that. She is waiting for everyone else to go first."

"What is she doing here?"

"I don't know. Randy's wife is still alive. I think so. Yes, I'm sure of it."

Her name escaped Zeke. She was one of those people that seem to be extras in the life of everyone else. Zeke berated himself for his callousness, but continued speaking, including Jerry in his coldheartedness.

"I can't remember her name."

"Nor can I."

"Do you ever feel that some people aren't real? Many people I mean. That they have no part to play but simply provide atmosphere."

"I do."

Zeke was surprised at Jerry's candor but then they were friends.

Jerry explained.

"Candace..."

"Is that her name?"

"I think so."

Jerry stepped to the mailbox mounted next to the front door and retrieved the Prentices' mail. He shuffled through the mail, stopping and smiling when he found confirmation of his memory.

"Yep, Candace Prentice. Someone thinks that she is real."

What he wanted to say what that Randy has Candace because a wife was expected. Like having a Bible in the house.

"You're worse than I am."

"We always have tried to outdo one another."

Jerry returned the mail to its box.

"It might be wiser to think of Candace as Randy did. I'm going to do that.

Its wrong, but less cruel. I take responsibility. It's my fault. I have a lower than normal emotional count limit. I'm surprised they don't measure it on blood work, like they do cholesterol. Its like a courtroom with limited capacity. I learned to ignore the outside world. Tell me Zeke, can you conceive of eight or ten billion unique people on this planet?

122

Zeke shrugged.

"Only a few people. Not billions. I can manage a few. The rest are props, less than extras. It's simpler for me and kinder to them."

"Is it?"

"It could be the other way round. In either case we've delayed enough."

Zeke moved toward the door, but his friend stopped him.

"Wait, you still haven't told me why Sybil Cochran is here."

"I don't know. If Candace was gone, I'd suspect that Sybil was here to bury and marry Randy."

"Don't you mean marry and then bury?"

Zeke shrugged again, and the two friends laughed together.

Randy Prentice was angry, and frustrated, and tired, and forgetful. He remembered clearly however that he was all of those things.

The stroke had rendered him weak, and he feared nothing so much as appearing weak and worse, ridiculous, in the eyes of other men. This made him angry, but even his anger was a pale copy of its previous self, the strong anger that was likely the origin of his stroke.

His younger self was a different person. Whoever said people don't change didn't live long enough to feel that he's just sprung from a cocoon. It was physical as well as mental. His skin had crystalized in places, like a low budget horror movie.

One day he had been normal, or passably so, the next day, his trusted mirror had verified the transformation. "Did a butterfly have the same sense of astonishment?" he wondered.

The world had slowed perceptively, it's sounds no longer rushed past his ears in an indecipherable torrent, or had it been only the diminished pounding of blood through his system?

Wind or blood, it mattered not which, as long as silence had returned.

There were chores to be done but they could, would need to wait.

He did not consider himself particularly observant. He wondered if anyone other than he had noticed the change.

He had changed but the world remained the same. Asleep it was the world which had changed while he had remained the same. It had been a dream, not just a dream from which he had awakened, but a dream too terrible to live and relive. Oh, to sleep and choose another less painful nightmare. To sleep, to dream, to awake, sane, healthy, human in the world that he knew as life. That was gone. Gone, but he clung to disbelief with a fervor that matched that of any, it mattered not, he prayed to any and all gods, hedging his pleas to the local favorite. One acquires and discards beliefs as readily as hobbies. Why him? Why now? Why? Why had he lived?

His nightmare returned each morning. He slept only to scream upon reawakening. His screams had grown silent, accustomed as he was to this neverending horror.

He was certain that he would be gone before the Holidays. He would escape that that evil time, a few weeks before Christmas when the majority of people were still recovering from their first bout of kindness. Normally generous folks were the worst, their fall so far that they failed to bounce at the bottom but ended up permanently damaged.

He thought again of his retirement, as he had so often recently.

It had been a relief, a welcome return to normalcy where money issues were minor concern. As to death, that was of no concern whatsoever as that would never happen to him. Of course, he understood that it would, but only in some distant, happy future. It would arrive suddenly, at the most convenient of hours, painless, unnoticed by himself.

The greatest of fears was nothing, for nothing defines her arrival, her breath on your face while your own stops forever.

Her gift was always the same, a nothingness that no one had successfully declined.

And then his son had been killed, in some place that unfortunately had not been godforsaken.

"Where?" he said aloud.

"Where?" Candace echoed.

"Randy, you start too often in the middle. I'm not there with you inside your head."

She felt herself a hitchkiker on a 40-year journey. The doorbell rang, offering a rest stop.

"Afghanistan," Randy answered after her unnoticed departure.

The ticking clock mocked him; soon, pause, soon, pause repeated endlessly. He sensed the minutes twist and twirl away, like dried oats in a dusty granary.

Randy's grandson was complaining, his nine-year-old high pitched voice piercing through the door of the master bedroom.

"That's it boy, complain. Maybe today is national complaint day. Let them know that you are alive," Randy whispered to the empty room.

"It's best to forget the dead, they would grant you the same courtesy, regardless of who are or imagine yourself to be. Complain boy."

Randy's stroke had derailed what he thought was going to be a smooth trip through life.

"What did it matter? Life was a solitary activity surrounded by other sole players."

Randy could do little but complain now, and that only feebly.

The door opened and in walked two men, they seemed familiar, but he did not remember their names.

"What was the boy's name? It was his grandson, so he would be called Randy. Wouldn't he?"

Young Randy was indeed complaining. He had discovered early that complaining to men was ineffective. Complaints to women was usually just as ineffective, but they tolerated it longer.

Today's grievance were the games at his mothter's side family reunion. They had left early to visit his father's parents. He would moan about that later.

"I don't understand this stupid game. They had us searching for things that we already have. What a waste of time."

"Randy means the family scavenger hunt," his mother explained to Cassie and Sybil and Candace.

"Your father used to really enjoy those hunts. One of the items collected might even have been his."

"I already have enough of his things at home. I miss him."

"So do I."

"I wish that he'd never left."

"So do I."

The boy turned toward Cassie.

"My father was killed in the war, in Overseas."

"Yes, I know, Randy. He was a good man."

"Soldiers go to Overseas all the time."

Sybil reflected on young Randy's words. Looking back, her childhood had been peace and her adulthood was war, war against anything, war for the sake of war, including war against war. And now it was war against peace. War for the sake of war. Peace was a better game. "Did they play that at family reunions," she wondered.

Cassie asked, "What are the men discussing in there do you think?"

The question took the boy unaware, and he stopped talking. He began to think.

"Hmmm," he marveled, "this was a good question. What were they discussing?"

Sybil spoke up.

"Men get together to discuss nothing. Believe me, I know men."

Cassie covered her mouth to hide her smile.

126

"Men have a curve; their emotions overrule their minds for decades. And then they claim that women are hormonal, too moody. Men are just permanently angry. And then, poof."

Candace stood, mumbled, "We need more coffee," and disappeared into the kitchen.

"They remain, for decades, primed and set like an unexploded bomb..."

Randy's mother gasped at the too near comparison, but Sybil remained oblivious.

"...ready to destroy the tranquility of summer passersby."

"Men outgrow it, they mature," young Randy's mother argued.

"Mature men, what a joke. They are so much the same. They are mental clones of each other."

Cassie added, "They are like drones circling a beehive."

Young Randy blurted, "I know about drones. They're good for blowing up terrorists. I saw videos."

"My God, what a world," Sybil exclaimed.

"And for sports, I like the Tour de France."

"It's all the same to him," his mother said in an attempt at explanation. "YouTube equalizes everything. Seeing everything is believing everything. Evil is not the enemy, but just another search category. What a world."

She stood quickly and hurried toward the kitchen.

"I'll give Candace a hand with the coffee."

A few minutes later, when Zeke and Jerry exited Randy's bedroom, all of the women were again seated together, young Randy sent outside to play, no batteries included.

Tension had lowered to a manageable level, with Sybil leading the discussion.

As he listened, Zeke grew annoyed that the topic was Linda and some supposed illness. Zeke chalked it up to the idle gossip at which Sybil excelled.

"If she isn't sick, she has no excuse not to participate in Brentville activities. Strolls around town don't qualify as membership. The back row doesn't lead."

Zeke and Jerry were reminded of Mrs. Cochran's lectures in high school, and they shared a glance together. Zeke was equally amused and irritated.

Sybil noticed the actions of her former students and raised her eyebrows in the manner the middle-aged men remembered so well.

"Her aloofness is a constant reminder of her status of outsider."

"Give her time, Sybil," Jerry countered, relishing the chance to call her by her first name.

"How much time does she need?" Candace said, claiming her position as hostess.

"More relevant, how much time does she have?"

"What does that mean?" Jerry asked.

"Cassie, what do you think?" Sybil asked.

"You are the expert."

Cassie straightened in her chair, pleased at the compliment.

"If she is sick, dying sick I mean, it's not like any cancer that I've heard of. She's thin, but she is not wasting away. She doesn't eat like an old cat of mine. She would feed constantly yet not gain an ounce."

All human events had their own human analogue in Cassie's world. Most people did not appreciate her comparison of the death of their spouse and the loss of one of her pets. For her part, Cassie chalked it up to human arrogance. Yes, she had been married once. It was a shame that men were a different species. Mixed marriages rarely succeeded. Cats were better.

The others in the room were unsure if the she was Linda or Cassie's elderly feline.

"She doesn't throw up. As far as I know."

The others nodded at this additonal piece of vagueness.

"In summary we don't know anything," Zeke said as way of conclusion.

"We know that she is a member of an invasive species."

"Which species?"

"Any of them that are different."

128

"Different than what?"

"Us."

The short answer could not have been more concise or more clear. No explanation of who us was, was needed.

"This woman, this so-called Linda Smith, whom has she latched onto? Mike Hayes and that Faulor girl, the town weirdos. It will end up in some cult."

Zeke began to object but Sybil plowed on.

In a way he enjoyed Sybil's monologues, they were always so memorable.

"Don't forget Zeke, Sybil," Jerry added in encouragement.

"An attorney. You know what I think of them."

Her audience nodded as one.

"Linda Smith and her merry band of oddballs are going to need an attorney before this is over."

"Before what is over?"

Sybil ignored the question as she had Zeke's previous attempted interruption

"And you," she nearly shouted to get his attention, then abruptly lowered her voice and enounciated, "Jerry goofball Yellowstone. What in the name of the good Lord is up with that? Yellowstone? You're borderline weirdo as well."

"Jerry is pushing to get into the cult, Sybil. He has asked me to draw up the paperwork."

"There, you admit it."

Sybil paused to gauge the mood of the room.

"Jerry never did have the sense of his father."

She swiveled to focus directly on target.

"I still remember your crazy uncle Carl. He should have stayed inWhitland. Get yourself a DNA test, Jerry."

"You jab me more than my recent allergy test."

"Sybil," he added, returning the prick.

"I have thick skin."

"I don't doubt it."

"The world is not as you want it to be. It was not ever how you want to pretend to remember it."

"It was," Sybil began.

"Not," the swift guillotine of his voice cut off further protest

129

"Not ever."

"I remember."

"Memory is a rusty chain that ties you down and poisons the blood."

Sybil wondered if that was from something that she had taught this boy so long ago.

"Memory is best ignored, forgotten one might say," Jerry went on.

"You can't learn much from the past, you'll do much better if you train yourself to forget."

"Forgive and forget, like Emily's father preaches," Zeke added.

"If you forget well enough the forgiveness will take care of itself."

"Why live at all, if you end up forgetting it all?

Cassie thought this was the opening she needed to suggest to Candace that now was the time for Candace to put her husband down, but on second thought it was probably better done in private. Sybil would probably be supportive, but she didn't believe that the others would accept the idea in the spirit offered.

"Jerry, that's crazy. I've taught enough students to identify the oddballs."

Jerry felt that he had spent enough time in Mrs. Cochran's remedial class. With another glance at Zeke, the two men stood as one, said their polite farewells, and left.

"Thank goodness they've left."

"More coffee?" Candace offered.

"Yes, please," the three other women said in unison.

It was time for serious talk, and that did not require the hostess' presence.

"I need a new kitchen," Sybil said.

"You can marry again. Its like repeating Freshman year in high school."

"Or a road trip. My nephew suggested one. If I pay, he will drive."

"Just the two of you?"

"One of us would kill the other, and I'm not as strong as I used to be."

Cassie looked at the other two women.

"We do need some men."

"You two have lost yours, Candace is about to lose hers, and I'm available."

She preferred not to dwell on her own history.

"I'm too young to be included in your coven," young Randy's mother said half jokingly."

"We are not witches, Jackie," Sybil admonished.

"If anyone is a witch, it is that Smith woman. She walks around town like some phantom with a fitness fetish. She is always in the cemetery. Why just the other day, she was there, all in black."

"Black in a cemetery?" Jackie asked rhetorically.

"She had no business being there. I asked her if she knew the deceased and she confirmed that she did not. It is as I told the men, they are still boys if you want my opinion, she in an invader. You'll notice how she has turned their heads, and that of Mike Hayes. They are men, I understand. And then there is that Faulor girl. There is going to be trouble."

"A cult?" Casssie inquired.

"Maybe. Women are generally too wise to be religious or to consider having been chosen by God to create yet another, pardon the pun, god awful religion. But the result is the same, women like to be in control."

"You would know," Jackie teased.

"Men don't appreciate it, but they come to accept that women are the final arbiters of behavior in society."

"Like knowing when its time for a new kitchen?"

"There is that."

"But you've remodeled more times than I can count, I've only done it once."

"But that is the same for each of us. It's been once per husband. I plan them like vacations so that I always have something fun to look forward to in the future. That way my bucket list is never completely crossed out."

"What do you mean?"

"Well, there was this one and the next one."

"There was Jack and..."

"And after Jack."

"Yes, and Afterjack."

"How many times have you been married, Sybil?",
Jackie asked.

"A few, some, several. More than one. Does it matter?
They weren't concurrent, if that's what is bothering you."

"Cochran was your first married name?"

"Yes, that is why so many of the grown kids still call me
that."

"And he died?" Jackie asked, wondering if this woman
had any advice for her.

"They died. I believe in til death do us part."

"Unhappy dead or happy dead is still dead. And you
missed one."

Jackie raised her eyebrows.

"You remember, Winston's excitable friend."

Sybil smiled at the memory.

"Let me tell the story."

"If you must," Sybil acquiesced, secretly pleased to hear
her history recounted.

"Winston was one of your husbands?"

Sybil nodded.

"Which one? Which number, I mean?"

"The most recent one. You miss a lot not living here,
Jackie. Are you moving to Brentville?"

"I don't know."

"I understand".

Having her audience's attention, Cassie began speaking.

"This is a funny story about Winston. Dead husbands
can certainly be drole."

"Really?" Jackie asked, shocked.

"Time heals all wounds, Jackie."

"I take your point; dying happy or dying unhappy is still
dying," Cassie added.

"So, getting back to Winston. He was well off enough
and retired."

"From what?"

"Once you're retired, retired from what becomes an
inane question. My patients have told me that so often that I

rarely mention it. It's like asking what were you before you were born."

"But," Cassie continued, taking a deep breath.

"After retirement, he continued with his past time of carpentry; he was really quite skilled. And modest. Modest, skilled, and probably decent in bed; I can see why Sybil married him."

"And why did Winston marry Sybile? Is she immodest, highly unskilled but spectacular in bed?"

"They say that opposites attract."

"Sybil you are quite the dark horse."

"Winston redid almost every wood fixture in their house, moldings, doors, cabinets. I never saw any of this until the day of Winston's wake; Sybil held it her house."

"Where is the funny part? So far it's more sad than humorous."

"Years before, Winston had a premonition that once he had finished the kitchen cabinets he was going to die."

"Like the woman owner of Winchester House?"

"Exactly. But for Winston he simply needed to do nothing; just simply not hang the cabinet doors. They remained in the basement for who knows how long, several years at least."

"You are telling me that these cabinet doors were complete, all finished and ready for hanging, but there they sat in the basement all because of a dream?"

"Yes. But despite his abiding by the 'rules'"

"Winston died anyway?"

"Yes."

"Where is the humor in that?"

"I'm coming to it."

"Ok, sorry."

"At the wake, in Sybil's house we were in the kitchen. It was crowded. Strangely, most of us had never been in the house before the day of the you know. But it was so easy for anyone to find cups, spoons, sugar."

Jackie nodded, picturing the scene.

"One of Winston's not close, creepy friends , Ian, wasn't it Sybil?""

Sybil nodded and said, "He wasn't creepy. A man can succeed being less intelligent or less ambitious; me, I learned to compromise. But boy, being both; that can be tough to overcome."

Anyway, this Ian, remarked that he'd be happy to come over some day the following week and install the cabinet doors for Sybil. We all knew what he really wanted to hang, Sybil included, but she was too polite to decline his offer."

"Don't tell me that they are now..."

"No," Sybil answered for herself.

Ian stopped by Sybil's the following week, went down to the basement and started to bring the doors up. He must have tripped and stumbled, for he fell halfway down the stairs and broke his neck."

"Dead?"

"Unhappy dead or happy dead is still dead."

"The doors are still in the basement?"

"Yes," said Sybil.

"That's why I need a new kitchen."

"And I need a new man. This is where we differ, Sybil. For you, men are consolation prizes."

"I suppose that you are still looking for Prince Charming."

"Its easier than before."

"Women don't outgrow their appreciation of eye candy, Jackie. Of course, a woman will disguise it well by saying that she is looking for her daughter, despite her own lack of children. You are either alive or dead. The senile, the demented, you've seen them. They are fearful, panicked at the loss of memory. Yet I wonder if we, the sane, aren't more fearful than the worst afflicted. We strive to retain what is only on loan. Alive or dead, that is the choice."

Sybil paused and looked directly at Jackie.\

"Regardless of your age or circumstances."

Jackie nodded slowly.

"Cassie works with the dying and the living most every day. She knows better than most. Alive or dead. Prudes have become an endangered species."

134

"You were married once, Cassie?"

"Yes, to a man named Paul. He defined the word couch potato. I had enough one day and hired some movers to come and haul away the sofa. With him on it, clutching the divorce notice."

"You're joking."

"That is what Paul shouted as they carried him out. Later on in court he referred to my action as the bitchkreig.

He really was the laziest man on Earth. He played at golf once every six or seven years, he was like a cicada in that respect.

"He sounds like my first husband and sex," Sybil said.

Jackie wished that Candace would return with the coffee, and perhaps some whiskey.

"Lloyd was such a miser, he rationed everything. Thank goodness that the school bus hit him early in his seven-year cycle. I did learn one thing from him."

"Men usually have much more to teach women."

"Lloyd was a golfer as well. He always shot par."

"That's impossible. Unless he cheated."

"Of course he did."

"Oh, I see. So, while he was on the green, you were playing through?"

"I wouldn't say that. Not yet. What I meant is that after each stroke,"

"Stop! I need a full cup before you continue. Where is that coffee?"

"After each club stroke, golf club stroke, he would proceed to where he intended the ball to go, not where it actually landed, or in his case I'm sure, where it watered. He called it a uni-scramble. He said that it took a lot of balls."

"I'm sure it did."

"But he was willing to use balls that weren't his. I took that statement as the one lesson that made sense to me. If he as a man was willing to use balls that weren't his, then I, as a mere woman, should be willing to use balls that weren't his as well."

"So much for fairytale endings. And where do you find your princes and frogs, Cassie?" Jackie asked, sure of the answer.

Sybil replied in Cassie's place.

"The internet. Where else? It's the local library filled with nothing but fashion and gossip magazine. It's a huge electronic high school, frozen in recess. What a wasteland."

Cassie shrugged as if to say, "What else is there?"

"I've looked there myself. Most of the men on it have contracted the web virus; they overvalue their worth. There, a boy or a man can opine on any subject without any knowledge whatsoever, and without ever have accomplished anything himself. Any all of this can do so anonymously. It's like driving drunk at night with neither license or lights."

"You have to be diligent in searching. You should appreciate Sybil, that you must do your homework."

"And no penalty. I dream of the day that I'll read of an idiot has been killed in a gruesome internet accident. I can see the headline now,

'Bombastic moron spills beer, found electrocuted 3 days later. Moment of jolt uploaded as deceased man's last act. Four million likes.'"

"Jackie, friends come and go. Husbands too. A few with regret, but through it all, and after the tears, after the anger, and yes, after the regret, you are stuck with yourself, your own imperfect deity. One you can't divorce or defriend no matter how much effort you devote to demolishing it."

"Until death do us part."

"That is not entirely true. Look around, these edifices are unanimous in claiming one truth; that you don't part from yourself even after death."

Jackie wondered how she had stumbled into such an intimate but useless conversation as this. Far better to help her with her next two weeks of loneliness.

"The funeral is still with me. And..".

There was too much add to state it all.

"I'm exhausted."

"Of course you are. At the same time what you say is utterly stupid. People are forced to live a reality that isn't there. I have my own reality, so do you, as does everyone. Where these collide is where we reside. It's a constant struggle made bearable by a combination of envy against the life of some and relief that we don't suffer the miserable fate of others. Get over it."

Jackie was shocked, as was Cassie.

"You're no help."

"I am helping. Your anticipated return to normal is not going to happen. Life is a one-way trip, no repeats and no staying in place."

"We both know that Sybil," Cassie said forcefully.

"Maybe. Your normal is now and forever different than it once was.

And don't get used to this new normal."

"God, I hate that term."

"Tomorrow will be familiar, recognizable. But there is no normal."

Think about it, I could not have spoken to you like this a month ago. You will get over this."

"I'll get over it."

"Yes, you will. But the scar will remain. Scars help, you know."

"Are they attractive? Will they make me sexy? Enough?"

"Everything on a woman is sexy to the right man."

Candace had remained in her drab kitchen, hoping that everyone would leave. Candace thought of poisoning the coffee. Her guests deserved to die; the annoying adolescent included. She poured sugar into its special bowl, wishing desperately that it was cyanide, or another, equally granulated deadly substance

But she had neither, only sugar, which would take decades to kill the occupants of her living room. Still, she could dream, as always. She had wasted her life. It was too late to change. Strange though, there was nothing to look forward to, nothing worthy of reminisence. Blankness in all directions, an endless fog in which it was easier to just sit down and wait. For whatever.

"How can women talk so much," he wondered. Aloud he said, "Thank God for televised sports" and turned on the television with the remote control.

A few minutes later he was even angrier and more annoyed.

"Foot volley on sand? Who dreamt up these bizarre sports? It was not as self parody as mixed doubles in table tennis had been.

Mixed doubles, ping pong?

It was madness beyond f'ing parody. They had towels to wipe their brows, after having moved less than a f'ing yard in the f'ing air-conditioned arena.

For some athletes their country might consider a loss literally sudden death.

What is mixed doubles anyway? What does that f'ing mean today. The entire f'ing world is f'ing mixed.

Me, I'm just mixed up." Randy finished his rant, neglecting to end it with his preferred adjective.

CHAPTER TWENTY-TWO

The boy arrived early in Brentville from Pittsburgh. Hannah had texted him the previous day, suggesting a meeting in town. She was a clever girl, she had not texted him the specific location, nor had she not provided him her home address. Hannah had not offered him anything. She had given him only desire.

The boy had arrived early, almost before the downtown area had wakened, cold air from the night would soon give way to the sun.

Gramps and his friends always stopped at the diner when they came on their fishing trips. It was only by accident that the boy had stumbled across the old part of town. He was amazed a drive-in still existed in the town. Gramps had told him about it, and he had plans to attend tonight with Hannah. That would be a fun thing to do from the past.

He imagined sometimes that he lived a century before, when crime paid, and the cops weren't so well equipped. It wasn't fair today for the criminal. He himself was proof of that.

The boy had strolled through town, this would have been his perfect base. "Instead," he began silently, but chose not to finish the thought.

Usually on the fishing trips to Brentville, the boy rode in back while his gramps drove and discussed world problems with one of his friends who sat in the front passenger seat.

In the rear, earbuds installed, the boy enjoyed the soft leather upholstery, its fragrance circulated quietly by the cool air that puffed from the numerous vents. It might just as well as have been a dusty concrete cell.

Today however he was the driver, and the expensive vehicle enveloped him like a tailored suit. The inside of the car was warm, the air sighed contentedly from vents front and rear, from overhead and underneath.

The air continued to exhale from the dashboard while the electrically heated seats encouraged him to remain in place.

He parked the car near the bakery, next to a white Honda minivan that was already there. He was careful to avoid ramming the right front tire into the curb as he pulled slowly into the diagonal parking place.

He left the vehicle, and upon closing it, a woman exited the bakery and made her way to the Honda, giving him a long glance.

"If she had been in charge of issuing maturity licenses, this creature would barely have a learning permit," she thought. "But he is cute."

He stopped and watched as she stepped into the van and slowly pulled away. She smiled and waved as she did so.

The boy waved back, noting as he did so that she too had avoided crushing a tire against the curb.

He turned west and began to walk slowly down main street.

The boy had no business in the courthouse, but he'd have enjoyed rotating the ancient cannon and sending one of its heavy, round balls through a wall of the century old courthouse.

The civil war cannon and monument to the of multiple wars adjacent to the courthouse demonstrated the everlasting struggle between the pessimism of age and the optimism of youth. Sometimes law is not the answer, and you need to act.

"Adults should really pay attention to what they teach outside of school," the boy said aloud, for the streets were nearly empty.

"Without weapons, actions are futile."

If only he could find some gunpowder, perhaps the next time up he would bring some of Gramps. Not too much, just enough to blast a hole in one of the walls. That would teach them to leave weapons laying around unattended. Adults needed lessons too.

Satisfied with his imaginary crime, he walked down to the stream that sliced through town. The boy stood motionless on the northern bank, watching downstream, where a middle-aged man practiced his casting. The man was younger than his gramps, but still he fished. Stupid. He probably had nothing better to do.

The boy thought of going to the tea shop, not for breakfast, as he had very little money, but for a cup of coffee. He would wait until Hannah texted him.

Linda slept late, emotionally drained, but forced herself to rise and begin her daily walk.

She decided to walk in the opposite direction, passing by the Catholic church, parallel to Main Street, which lay invisible, obscured by trees.

Cobblestone and brick surfaced a few streets, and on Pickering, cottages stood, roofed in slate. The sight never failed to halt her steps. Eyes closed, Linda could nearly convince herself that she heard the clip clop of horse hooves. Particularly on a day when the fog had not yet lifted. She had probably missed such a morning today by oversleeping.

She walked along Tunnel Road, and then turned left, toward downtown and the tearoom.

A firetruck passed her quietly, out for its own daily constitutional. It carried a flag on its rear deck, some sort of police/fire variant of the national banner. When had the firemen switched allegiance she wondered, glad that her possessions were fireproof and that her house, well it wasn't hers. Was that how the firemen felt about the country? "Then why not resign," she asked herself

Before she crossed the bridge, she saw Zeke fishing in North Fork, near the softball field.

Linda altered her route, trotting across the diamond to say hello.

It took a bit of waving and shouting before Zeke noticed her presence. He retrieved his line and walked over to join her.

"How are they biting?"

"If they knew what I was doing, they might decide to chew on me directly."

"What are you doing?"

"I'm not fishing, only casting. I'm not hoping to hook anything, not a trout anyway. I enjoy the sound of rushing water, and the sense of being out of touch in the middle of town. Its being lost in a town that is lost to the world. I like it, now and again."

"I've been watching. Your casts are wonderful."

"Careful now there Linda, you're making a grown men blush."

Zeke showed her the line, there was no hook attached. "See, no tricks."

Upstream, Hannah was upset.

Her magical place felt strange.

There were a few anglers and the odd detector milling about, for at this time of year they were as common as hummingbirds.

The running water had its familiar numbing yet soothing tone, and the overhead hiss still called her name. Hannah kicked at a mound of shale debris that lay at one of the feet of the massive concrete pillars that supported the bridge span.

The immense bridges of the interstate were painted green in order to blend in. Or was it done to obscure their value as an escape route, Hannah pondered.

Hannah gazed again at the overhead concrete, compelling in its drabness

She bent over and scooped up handful of the pebbles, regarding them as she had the book in Linda's living room yesterday.

But her magical place's sense of seduction was diminished today. Because of Linda. Their petiteness reminded Hannah of her own nothingness and she cast them away. They landed like a flock of small, dark geese on the flowing water, but then disappeared silently, their disappearance obscured by the sound of the stream and the overheard traffic.

"That will be you," a voice said. Hannah spun around, expecting to see Mary. But she was alone.

The discussion from the other day had aggravated the panic that was raising in her body like a spring flood. Indeed, the future was passing her by like an uncaring chauffeur of a luxurious time machine. The interstate passing overhead was a statement in concrete as to her town's insignificance. The gray ribbon blasted across the ravine at a distance of less than one half of one mile. Brentville lacked the worth to merit an inexpensive bypass but instead was overridden.

The people, her neighbors had been bypassed before the freeway arrived, decades ago. They were second and third generation castaways. Her fellow prisoners thought themselves blessed hermits.

Linda had preached in the cemetery that "The past dies unless you sprinkle it periodically with visits from the future. That is us, we make those visits."

In Hannah's experience, to uncaring strangers Hannah was as good as dead and buried. They passed over her grave at above the posted limit, what concern had they for anyone other than themselves.

Oh, how she wanted to be just like them, these uncaring strangers who led irresistible lives.

Linda was so wrong about so much.

The university of the world; it was her creation. It offered an education requiring neither debts nor tests.

The vehicles above contained students and alumni alike of that creation.

She had no intention of remaining in this town and putting down deeper roots. Those she had needed to be yanked out while still shallow enough to not anchor her here forever.

It seemed already to be forever, seventeen years, that was a generation. A generation wasted, how many more of them had she, four? Five?

What she did need was money. She had a so-called job. Several jobs in fact. A waitress and a checkout girl. What a spiteful term she hissed aloud, for there was no one nearby to hear her words. The hiss went upward, blending into those sent down from the tires of strangers' cars. They agreed with her; it was a spiteful term.

Linda. She was another disappointment, an uncaring stranger who had deigned to stop and deliver the insult in person, "I can help with a used car."

Her thoughts turned to the boy.

"Her boyfriend," the word sounded foreign on her lips. Boyfriend described him as poorly as another word she could have selected. It would do for the short term that she would have need of him. He was not a means to an end; he did not rise to that level. He was at most a means to a means.
    He provided transportation and a few secondhand anecdotes that might be of value.
    Her would be paramour had suggested a trip to Pittsburgh. Despite her overwhelming desire to leave, as any burgh would do, she rejected his transparent ploy immediately.
    It was time to text the boy. She was miserly with her texts for the device could be as annoying a leash as any man, or boy. The phone had become the tool of a voyeur, to watch the life of another human unfold, like those speeding by even now overhead. A detector had shown her once how his own leash, a metal detector worked. It was simple really, but what had stayed with Hannah had been his description of the junk he had unearthed, "relics, Hannah, relics from another time."
    Consolation prizes for those who don't find pots of gold, Hannah had told herself.

She grew up on the information highway road filled with unlicensed drivers, reckless drivers, oblivious drivers all prone self-righteous road rage. Overhead the traffic passed by on the interstate. Each occupant content in their ignorance of her existence. If only she could travel as easily in the real world as readily as she did online.

She would shed this life, eighteen years buried underground was long enough, too long, longer than the cicadas that would hatch this year or next. She would beat them to life, she thought, smiling to herself, a smile that they quickly straightened, not wanting to lure any of the anglers from their cold, watery passion.

Hannah texted the boy a location a few minutes walk away, as this magical place, for it had resumed its magic in a brief few minutes, was not for a boy.

CHAPTER TWENTY-THREE

Hannah had consented to the boy coming to the house for their first date. His grandfather's car was nice, and for once, Hannah did not want to walk.

He had been amazed that drive-ins still existed, commenting that his Gramps had told him all about drive-ins. Its name, The Moonlite drive-had been as irrestistibles as Hannah.

She had been fearful, but more terrified of being afraid. She would face it directly. He was a second rater, definitely not first string. Yet he could be dangerous or useful. A perfect first match. She would have home field advantage and the implicit support of the town. Plus, she would take her knife, a rare gift from her father.

One of the first things he had said had been "You don't talk like the other people around here."

She soon discovered that this would be his only meaningful observation. Hannah had worked diligently to lose her accent and constant contact with it served as a reminder of her efforts to break yet another restriction imposed by a vanished generation.

Hours later, during the short ride back to her home, a prison within a prison, Hannah was mildly disappointed that she had not needed to display let alone use the knife. It had remained tucked away, unbloodied.

If she had sliced the boy...why had she such difficulty remembering a single name, she would have cut off her own plan before it began. Getting caught for a crime provided no credibility, that was a self awarded consolation prize for bunglers. Hannah had no intention of being caught.

Linda was right, think and then act. Both were important. Mary Parks would never learn that lesson. And Emily? Well, that was Emily's choice.

If the thought was big enough, sufficiently clever, the action would deliver itself. Or so Hannah theorized.

One big idea, like those men in Silicon Valley had. Why was it always men who enjoyed moments of genius? In other circumstances she would have discussed the conundrum with Linda, but that door was closed. Or was it? Probably. She had no desire to reopen it. Not tonight, and not tomorrow.

Hannah's thoughts returned to the here and now, anticipation of the then and future.

"One idea, one action," she said aloud. Not using the knife, yes, that had been a blessing. The film was weak, as was her so-called date. The boy had added nothing of value to her life. She would not see him again. There was no point, for either of them. He was a self-confessed incompetent. Still, she listened to him, perhaps she could learn something from his numerous mistakes.

She would much rather have driven out, in the time it took for the movie to run its predictable course, they could have crossed the state line in three directions. But not with the boy.

The film had been terrible, if there had been a plot, it must have been dropped from the final product, forgotten among the need to add nudity, vulgarity, violence, and shrill preaching, all the ingredients for a modern masterpiece.

It resembled nothing so much as a story from the Old Testament that her grandfather had so enjoyed. The adjective old had been the only word that Hannah had needed to hear to discard the dead scripture.

Hannah laughed at the idea of her grandfather, instead of her, sitting next to the boy, the two of them enjoying the film. The boy's name no longer mattered; it was one less bit of the past to forget.

Men, she understood them now. They loved both the past and unrealistic futures, either the same fairy tale, repeated over and over and over, endlessly, or one wrapped in shiny, colorful, new paper, but just as simplistic.

Hannah thought suddenly of the one boyfriend of her mother, the only one worth keeping. But her mother had botched that. After so many lumps of coal, perhaps she had been unable to recognize a genuine diamond. She was no detector, that was for sure.

The man had been interested in the museum at Cool Springs. Once, while waiting for her mother, the two of them had enjoyed a real conversation.

"I picked it up as a hobby," the older man had said to Hannah.

"It was inexpensive, and the technology was simple, a few steps up from a bicycle, or was it the other way round? It doesn't matter I suppose.

Over time it became what all male hobbies become, an obsession centered around equipment."

"Like the anglers," Hannah thought now as she sat silent next to her own boyfriend. Men were so slow at times. She wondered if men were somehow visually impaired as nature's attempt at equalizing the sexes.

"It became all about bragging rights, if you can believe it, over who had the most impressive piece of archaic iron," came the words from last year.

"It's harmless enough, I guess. Ridiculous, definitely."

"Men are silly," Hannah had said to her mother's date, the words eliciting a knowing nod of the head.

"As are women. Seriousness is reserved to the silliest among us."

Those magical men in Silicon Valley, they thought like women, but acted with the arrogance and singlemindedness of their fellow gender. If they could channel their femininity and succeed, she could do the inverse. She could pole vault as well as they did. She had achieved her track goals inverted, where upside down was right side up.

Hannah recalled a conversation she had once with Emily's father, the last conversation of any consequence. He had given a sermon derived from the book of wisdom, after which she had asked him why did he preach from any of the other sections? He had no answer.

The ending notes of The Weeknd's Blinding Lights brought her back to the present. The car had stopped. She was home, for now. She smiled broadly, the date had been fantastic, she exclaimed, despite your presence, she kept to herself.

He leaned over to kiss her, but she opened the door. The warm airflow increased at the drop in pressure, a final plea to not leave. The boy leaned back in his seat, defeated.

Hannah leaned over, kissed him, and sprang from the car before he could react.

The boy had had a few bucks, from Gramps no doubt, enough for a hotel room, and some entertainment. He'd have been better off sleeping in his car, because she had no intention of visiting his room. It was probably one that she had cleaned many times when she had worked as a maid for six months. She made more in tips at Shay's in a day than in a week as a sheet changer

Hannah smiled again and lied. "It was wonderful, lets do this again," not pausing to guess his name.

She would never see him again. Sooner or later one of them would push the other to a fatal fall.

As the door swung closed behind her, she heard a new song begin, Broken, by Lovelytheband.

"Another foolish, if catchy tune," Hannah reflected as the door closed with an expensive thud.

CHAPTER TWENTY-FOUR

Zeke and Linda met for dinner in the café, preferring to dine downstairs at the small table furthest from the bar.

"Its so calm here, I feel as if I snapped my fingers and froze time."

"Haven't we already done that according to Hannah Faulor?"

"What is Hannah's story?", Linda asked, touching the back of Zeke's left hand.

"Other than being young and bored? It happens all the time."

At least once during their encounters, Linda had taken to touching Zeke; on the shoulder, his hand, his forearm, it mattered little where. It proved that he, and she, were still real. Zeke never mentioned it but sometimes reciprocated her actions.

"She must be a toucher," Linda expected that Zeke thought.

Did today's girls satisfy the same need with their smartphones, someone or something who would tolerate the most unexpected of caresses?

"Hannah used to clean for me."

"I clean for myself."

"It helped her with some cash, and she kept me informed. More or less."

"Ah, a snitch."

"That was my plan, but she wasn't very good at it. Or maybe there was nothing to tell."

"I doubt it, there is always something to tell with teenage girls."

"Probably. More or less became less and less."

"Maybe you didn't pay her enough."

"Maybe not. I wanted to get ahead of any issue that might come up that involved her or one of my nieces. I saw her, and still do, as another niece. She really has no one else."

"What is your interest?"

"I'm not sure. A desire to help, a way to be vicariously eighteen, curiosity, all of the above. With a bit of jealousy thrown in."

Zeke scoffed, "You, jealous?"

"Speaking with someone of her age can be intimidating. She is two people, a girl and a woman. It's like first contact with an alien life form. I'm far removed from her, our cultural reference points don't overlap and if I attempt to use those with which she is familiar, I feel foolish, like an inept spy who is simply sent home by the enemy out of pity. Even our language is different. I don't want to come across as condescending to her."

Zeke abruptly changed the subject.

"Let's go to the dance together. Its in six months so plan ahead. It will be either cold and dry, or cold and wet. It gives you time to find the perfect dress.

"It gives you time for lessons, too."

"I'm hurt that you confuse me with Jerry."

Zeke noticed the doubt in her eyes.

"The tango is a dance impossible to master and impossible to forget."

"Perfect. I take it that you don't have much in the way of a wardrobe."

"No, but I can find something if I need to."

"It is easy for you, you're rich. As a rule, I refuse to date rich women."

"You have everything, travel, adventure, a mysterious past. Probably an alias or two."

"Except youth. Hannah had said it about Zeke the other day. 'He lacks youth.' So do I, even more so.", Linda reflected.

"I'm not rich" she responded.

"Believe me Linda, you are rich."

Before she could protest further, he added,

"Of course, I have a low definition for being rich and most women pass my threshold. Figuratively speaking. I've had to compromise my virtue, you understand. So to speak. I would be delighted to accompany you to the dance."

Linda smiled at Zeke's affrontery.

"I would never have guessed that you were an attorney."

"I still am."

"Yellowstone will be disappointed, but I'm sure that he can find someone else. Someone young and appreciative of what he has to offer."

"I have no doubt of it

"He'll find someone. I can't have been his first crush."

"A first crush is like a dead wife, you can't compete, they grow more perfect by the day."

"Oh?"

"Sorry. His wife died."

"He said that she was controlling. I took that to mean they had divorced because she was too controlling."

"Jerry needed to be controlled. Like I said, he is emotional."

"Too controlling or nothing," Linda remembered.

"Emotion is a valuable tool, too precious and powerful to deploy every day. It needs to be reserved for special occasions. Jerry has problems in that regard. He has lived his life as if on stage, court was perfect for him. Outside the courtroom, nothing was real, yet every utterance was meaningful. Let me correct myself, it wasn't that nothing was real, it was rather that everything was more than real."

Zeke changed the conversation again.

"I stay away from young girls. They are dangerous."

"Hannah?"

"Yes," Zeke shrugged in respone. He could have been referring to any young female.

"It goes both ways, I suppose."

"I'm not sure if women become more or less dangerous as they age. None of them are ever harmless. In Hannah's case, I wised up before she could snitch on me."

"What would she say?"

152

"Does it matter? See, you're ready to believe anything when in fact there was nothing. Not even very good housecleaning. She's cornered, or she sees herself cornered, trapped in a cage."

"That's interesting. She and I were talking of lives in cages. I meant to tell her that Hell is not other people."

"Huis Clos."

Linda looked at him, surprised.

"No Exit," he said.

"Sorry."

"Your expression was apology enough. What did you tell Hannah?"

"Well, "Linda continued after gathering her thoughts, "I said that Hell is not other people, its not having enough other people. With a larger cast it would have been a comedy."

"How many more?"

"Oh, I don't know. Thousands?"

"If you were to stage it here, it would be what, a tragedy? Our theater is not that large."

"The whole of Brentville is a stage. It is anything but a tragedy."

"I'm serious."

"About what?"

"About staging a play, that is if you are staying for a, not that I'm asking,".

"You have the same expression that I must have had a moment ago when you mentioned Huit Clos. That makes us even."

"I guess that it does. You know Linda, we do have a theater group in town. We are somewhat of a tourist attraction, if you haven't noticed. We are always looking for draws."

"I'm here to relax not to work."

"Work can be relaxing. For me it's my deerstand. You will have to visit me there sometime."

"In the winter, when it is cold?"

"No, silly, when it is warm, like this coming weekend."

"Deer season is not for months. Hmm, I sense that I'm being stalked myself."

"I'm sorry, I don't..."

Linda winked.

"I'm an adult Zeke. I can take care of myself. I've been hunted before. What about you? There are plenty of women in town?"

"I wanted to give you a chance, your being new to the area. I take my role as unofficial welcome wagon very seriously."

"I appreciate your efforts. Maybe."

"Maybe what?"

"Maybe on a play. I only need to freeze it for a while longer."

"Until you move on."

"Maybe."

"Oh," he uttered, disappointed

"Or maybe not. "

"How long is a while longer?"

"I'd like to stretch it long enough so that I can forget the future. I settled here not to escape the past but the future."

"You have no idea what the future is."

"That is what makes it terrifying."

Linda invited Zeke for a nightcap after dinner, and they walked the short distance to her home.

"I went to a town meeting the other day."

"You ventured to Livetown?" Zeke teased, referring to the new part of Brentville, where the chamber of commerce conducted meetings when they met outside of the district.

The discussions they held frequently devolved into arguments that all participants understood to be essential. For to have nothing worth arguing over would indeed be a sad state of affairs.

Linda had forced herself to attend only as a result of her newly hatched sense of civic duty. She was not convinced that it would survive adolescence.

"Did you sign up for anything," Zeke asked lightly.

"No, not yet."

"That's ok. You have plenty of time."

Once inside, Linda led Zeke into the kitchen to select a wine.

"There is some in the refrigerator, if you prefer chilled."

154

"I see that you have wine and wine, some vegetables, some sort of sauce,"

"Its my own sauce, by that I mean that I purchased it all by myself."

"It must go well with vegetables, or is it the wine? "No cheese? Oh, that's right."

Linda had given up trying to either correct or track down where this idea of her being a vegan originated.

"Since we've already eaten, just wine is fine. You'll have to issue me a raincheck on the sauce and other items."

They took their glasses of wine into the living room.

"I didn't realize that Mrs. Dietz was such a reader. Or are these books all yours?"

"Not a one. I wonder if any of Jerry's are here."

"If you find one, save it. They are great for starting fires."

"Is that the sound of jealousy?"

"Jealousy is the most valuable of human traits. Its victimless, any injunction against it arbitrary and itself a crime against our nature."

"This wine could have used more filtering," Zeke commented.

"I have other bottles."

"I'm kidding Linda, the wine is fine. I just wanted to change the subject."

"Jealousy or regret. I burned my old journals a while ago. All the years of my diaries blazed in a few minutes" Zeke said.

He stepped to the bookcase and selected a tome at random.

"The secret of life in twelve easy steps. Or not," he added, replacing the random piece of fiction in its slot.

"Life is the only fiction that counts. It's the only game we humans play that has no winners. It is Simon says where we all fail, any victory ephemeral, erased by subsequent players."

"Six months ago, I was positive that life had derailed me but instead it switched me to a different track, one I had not ridden on before. Now, I see that life is a single track, regardless of what levers we imagine that we are pulling.

"Hmm," was his noncommittal reply.

He thought more, then added "Life arrives without warranty, like any gift."

"Sometimes I wonder if the new acquaintances are actual people, or if they appear in response to my thoughts. They magically materialize and then grasp and make their own lives from that moment forward.

I feel the same way about you right now at this very second. Were you here a moment ago?" she asked, reaching over to run her hands down from his shoulders to his fingertips.

"You are real enough I suppose," Linda decided.

"Good luck," she said a moment later.

"With what?"

"In case I'm wrong and you're one of the newly created. I'm afraid that you are on your own."

"Jerry expressed a similar idea the other day."

"Is that good or bad?"

"It just is. You may not know this, but he and I are distant cousins. When we were kids, we had an uncle Carl. My parents kept him at arms length, and I don't think that many people knew of our relationship.

"In Brentville? I've been here only a brief time, but I already know things that I probably should not."

"Such as what?"

"We will leave that for another day."

"Are you sure?"

"Yes, I'm sure. Tell me about Carl."

"My uncle Carl, crazy Carl the family called him behind his back, told me on numerous occasions that sanity is overrated. Maybe he was right. Reality goes better with a twist of fantasy."

"What happened to him?"

"Oh, the usual. They took him away, but that was back when they did take people away, like trash they likely thought at the time. Hide it away before it caused a stink."

"That's harsh."

"Nowadays they just recycle these people, they wash and polish them and then repeat the process when they do begin to stink. Is that less harsh?"

"Everyone has difficulties."

Zeke laughed.

"Most people have problems. Your problem is that you think you have problems. You don't have problems."

"But I do."

"But you do have concerns, worries. You worry too much."

"I know, but I can't help it. This is my nature."

"And I solve problems." He pulled a half empty box of matches from his jacket pocket.

"Write down your worries here on this sheet of paper and I will put in this box along with my solution here. He reached into his jacket pocket, the left side this time, retrieved something after a moment of searching, and placed it quickly in the worry box

"What was that?"

"Don't worry about it," he said with a wink.

He then placed the box back in his jacket pocket.

"We will check these together in a week, maybe two depending on the temperature. You have up to a fortnight now worry free."

"Promise me that you won't look until then."

"I promise."

Zeke selected another, heavier book, one filled with photographs of paintings.

"I was wrong."

"About what?"

"This wine is very good, Linda. It just needed a few minutes to warm up."

"I'm glad that you're enjoying it."

"Do you see these photos, this one, the Mona Lisa? They never show the rear side, where it is just gray canvas, the same as millions of other unknown paintings."

Linda took the book from his hands.

"I've always wondered about the still life; you know those oil paintings by the old masters that show unkempt scenes. Upset pitchers and unarranged fruit. Where was the housekeeper? She would not have permitted such a mess. Its staged."

"And these other books? These are dead wood. Literally. They are two dimensional."

Linda chose one, Blue Highways.

"I partially read this decades ago. This is worthy of being started, but more worthy of not being read in its entirety. Travel books, like the voyage they recount, are better left unfinished by the reader."

"Tell me more about your voyage."

"It was my voyage. Life is solitary confinement, even at the best of times."

Zeke could not bring himself to dispute the point.

"It required two decades, 20 years after having left California, for me to realize that being self centered is not a vice but a worthy goal. Philosophers urge us to know oneself, I suggest be yourself. It really is all about you. Just be polite about it, if only for the sake of self preservation. Why worship a golden calf when for a fraction of the price you can purchase a fine, silver backed reflecting glass."

"Do you mean this?"

"To a degree. You have no one to deliver you except yourself."

"That's very dogmatic."

"My father advised me when I was still in high school that you can't shame a cheap man and you can't reason with a zealot. For both, their self perceived virtues provide strong armor. Which are you, Zeke?"

"Neither. I am an ordinary man. I have no virtues, unless you count honesty and humility. As far as vices, I use my cellphone too often. I carry this 10-foot green cord and this adapter. It's a combination lifeline and spare tire."

"It keeps you anchored?"

"Exactly," he agreed proudly, ignoring her sarcasm

Zeke noticed the absence of a television. He saw no computer or cellphone.

"You don't like electronics, I see."

"Its mutual dislike. Machines of old, like those over in the historical society's museum, might tear your arm off if you ventured to close, but they wouldn't manage every moment, waking or asleep, of your life, from some unpeopled data center on another continent. It's worse than a return of Greek gods. I have enough want to be gods in my life. And the pain, actual pain."

Shen saw the doubt in his eyes.

"They are not satisfied with our best efforts; they prod us mercilessly. I suffered apple aches," Linda said with a grin.

"How did we get on these topics? I don't usually talk like this, or this much."

"What are apple aches?"

"Headaches, unaccustomed neck pain, wearied eyes. The symptoms are identical to those experienced by those with the Samsung variant. So I fled the electrictrified church. I'm much happier since I abandoned the faith, healthier as an apostate."

"Healthy is good."

Linda said nothing.

"It is as I told you the other day Linda, we have it all here. Arts, writing, publication, all local. Even the paper."

"You don't have to sell me on the town. It's a supportive town."

"Support is a two-way street."

"You're referring to the play again?"

"I'm talking about a play, or a pageant, or a paddle down North Creek. Something that you could organize. I see you reading about our town, notice I said our town, Linda. We have a balance of yesterday, and today, and tomorrow."

"The past and the future," Linda whispered, the sound a faint echo.

"And the present, don't forget the present Linda. We could you a little bit more of tomorrow is all that I am saying. We can talk about that".

"Tomorrow."

Linda slammed the book closed and then reopened it. She bent to the open page and inhaled.

"It's intoxicating," and passed the opened book to Zeke.

"Nostalgia? I prefer other intoxicants," and closed the book.

"A still life by Rembrandt is attractive, buts it is 400-year-old dry paint, not an actual orange. I'm not willing to give up the third dimension."

"I guess you're right. But one can't collapse in a two dimensioned world, there is no down, no place to fall. Is that so bad?"

"Brentville strikes you as two dimensional? That is a horrible way to describe the people that live here, including you and me."

"It is horrible, I plead guilty".

"Your honor," she added in an attempt at humor she saw as failed the moment that she uttered the two words.

"Its not funny."

"I need simple."

"For how long?"

"Linda," Zeke said, you are behaving the same as the sheriff from Rose Hill. You are capturing and documenting the lives and memories of strangers."

"They are worth preserving."

"Perhaps, but to what end? These lives and memories aren't yours. They won't become yours, no matter how much you try."

"No matter how hard you scrub ones past it won't wash off, it doesn't rinse."

"I know that. I told you that Jerry's wife died. So did mine."

Linda caught her breath.

"Counting the days, weeks, months since my wife's death does nothing to relieve the pain. It brings back my best memories that I know will only reside in the past. The past for me is different I think than it is for you, Linda. She and I will have no more fresh memories and the images that I possess will fade over time. I want fresh memories."

"And I want what at one time constituted a normal existence; small town, village life. Just big enough with just enough people. No exit."

CHAPTER TWENTY-FIVE

For their hike, Zeke had suggested jeans, eliciting a laugh from Linda.

"I don't do jeans."

Instead, she wore the khaki slacks relegated to gardening and other earthy adventures.

Linda walked to the teashop for a jolt of caffeine before their expedition.

Somehow the tea was more delicious went brewed by anyone other than herself. She sat and relaxed, her back to the door, it was less distractive in that position, and she treated herself to a second cup before using the restroom.

Linda observed the white minivan as she stepped from the café late one morning.

It was not an uncommon vehicle. She had observed this one or it's twin, several times over the past few weeks.

The car's appearance was an unwelcome reminder that Linda had a past future, a warning that her present past was maintained precariously.

It was a vague threat of being yanked back into the future. It rolled into Brentville and into her view rarely and randomly. The very haphazardness of the sightings added to her uneasiness. She wanted to embed herself in this tiny plot of soil. Maybe someone would steal the car. Or the owner might sell it on. It was a trifle, a pebble in her shoe that she should learn to ignore.

Surely it could not be her own former Odyssey. On a whim, she strolled over to the car and stepping to the rear, looked downward to see a temporary Pennsylvania tag. It sat within the same bracket that had once held a Delaware plate. It was indeed her former Honda.

Linda frowned.

She had sold this very machine the day that she had relocated to Brentville. It had been a quick and painless separation. Linda had consigned the van to its fate, one that she did not envision entailed it remaining, in all it's hearse-like purity, as a periodic premonition of death. She had an excess of those already.

Linda moved over to the driver side door and peered in through the window, curious as to the new owner. Was she, Linda entertained no possibility that the driver was male, an attorney doing attorney stuff in the courthouse across the street? Was she simply in town, running errands or shopping? Was she dining in the café this very minute?

Linda peered through the driver's window, curious as to the identity of the new owner. It was pristine. There was no babyseat, no miscellaneous materials on the floor or in the second row, nothing to distinguish this white van from the one that she had left at the local Chevy dealer a few months ago.

The keys were in the ignition. Thank goodness the keychain was not the one she remembered turning in, otherwise she might have had an anxiety attack.

She laughed at the thought. An anxiety attack.

Linda had grown up poor, her family could not afford anxiety attacks, they had to settle for basic fear, a commodity that had been in constant oversupply.

She could now acquire as much anxiety as she desired, a level that she now put at zero. She was living in Brentville as an antidote to fear, and worry, and to anxiety.

"And to life," a nagging voice sounded in an annoying squeal.

The squeal became the sound of rubber on concrete, as Zeke came to a halt beside her, his cross-trainers wailing in complaint.

"It's only a car," she said aloud before Zeke was able to say anything.

"What?"

"Nothing."

"Ready?"

162

It was the same question that he had posed to Emily the other day. It was the perfect question to lighten Linda's mood, and she suddenly felt eighteen again.

A few moments later, Cassie crossed the street from the bakery, stepped into the Odyssey and drove off towards Summerville.

"Brentville is such an oasis from the world," Cassie thought, not for the first time.

CHAPTER TWENTY-SIX

"Let's halt for a moment, Linda."

They stopped, but Linda remained standing, convinced that sitting encouraged deception.

"This is a good spot for a photo, Linda."

"I'll just save it in my mind. I left my electronics at home. I like the sound of that, 'home'. I've given up on these gadgets. Taking a loaded smart phone on a walk is little different than taking a chaperone on an expectant date."

"Is that what this is?"

"A walk?"

"Not an expectant date?"

The trail extended for many miles, cutting through towns, skirting isolated farmhouses, meandering through sun dappled woods. Today, the trail was empty of other hikers. At one point, Zeke mentioned that the area that they had just traversed had been a dairy in the distant past.

Linda marveled at the variety of plants and trees. And the sound of birds and insects. It was all song, a thousand ways to chant existence.

"I've taken up gardening, with the help of Mike and Emily. It is quicker than planting a tree and waiting a century."

"There are more than enough trees around us Linda. What is one less? Still, you don't go out of your way to leave a mark. Except for one."

"Oh, which is that?"

"I've seen your bathroom."

"I haven't seen yours," Linda whispered coyly, and then laughed.

"It's exceptional, my bathroom that it, but it's not my work."

"Maybe not, but it could have come from your hand. It's new and different, but classy. You are fortunate that we have talented local artists. Plus, you had to compete with the couple renovating. Krall House. They are painting everything, redoing and installing bathrooms, renovating at least five bedrooms across three floors. I may have left something out."

"How long has that been going on?"

"Too long or not long enough. Depending on who you ask, the home was either ruined, nothing more than a ruin, or in the process of becoming a ruin. But it is back or soon will be. The couple is also involved in every facet of the town, church, chamber of commerce, attractions.

It is going to be spectacular again. I'm sure that they are going to succeed. The hall lay prostate years ago, almost in need of medical attention. Perhaps it did. It deserved to be saved.

Brentville as a whole merits saving, preserving the portion of the past that is significant, while advancing it to where, heck I don't know. To the future, some future, to a sort of life. That is the best that I can offer."

"You are truly passionate about Brentville."

"So are you, you just won't admit it to anyone except yourself."

Linda's silence affirmed his words.

"It is a struggle to keep the town moving forward at a pace that does not bulldoze what has been built and is worth preserving. It needs to be done slowly."

"When did you see it?"

"Just the other day, when I stopped by to discuss some committee work."

"When did you see my upstairs bathroom?"

Zeke stammered.

"I haven't seen it exactly. Emily has. Remember the day when she slid down the banister?"

Linda nodded and smiled at the memory.

"She described it to me. Emily has an eye for detail."

"I like that memory; it makes for a good story to relive."

"Hey," Linda exclaimed.

Zeke looked at her expectantly.

"What did I do now?"

"Speaking of stories."

Zeke remained silent.

"You haven't told me your milk story."

"Milk story?"

"Don't you remember?"

Zeke did remember, he wanted to hear Linda recount their encounter.

"At our first meeting, at Hannah's and Emily's track meet, you said that you would tell me your milk story one day."

"I did say that," Zeke confirmed, his voice pleased with Linda's recollection.

"Today is one day, and the setting seems appropriate for a milk story."

"It is indeed, Linda. This is a fine spot. Let us sit upon the ground and tell stories of glasses of milk."

"It's a childhood memory. I'm not sure why I spoke about it that day. It just popped into my head. A glass of milk, it sounds trivial, silly. Anyway, here goes a glass of milk.

The most vivid of memories can arrive unbidden, forcing their way into consciousness despite deliberate attempts to forget them or the simple passage of time.

The most mundane of actions, including those performed a single time, can imbed themselves as precise remembrances in one's storehouse of all that combines to create our reality.

They can be triggered by a sight, a sound, an odor.

For me it was a glance at a piece of furniture in my home.

It was one of those inexplicable mysteries that anchored in my brain the pedestrian experience of drinking a glass of milk one July evening, many years ago, in a Pennsylvania farmhouse

I was seated, along with my two older siblings on the bench, a plain, homemade set of wooden planks, painted in white, not oyster, or ivory, but white. The seating surface was covered in what we called contact paper, but which was more or less an adhesive backed shelving paper. It had the advantage of facilitating sliding as we sat and exited en masse with little danger of acquiring a sliver in the rump.

Placed between the massive, thick-legged kitchen table and the wall, beyond which lay the cellar stairs.

The bench accommodated three or four children and was our preferred place for meals as we had nothing like it at home.

I myself had such fond memories of it this bench seat that years later, I convinced my wife of the indispensability of such a piece.

One was duly acquired, sadly it had to be more elegant, for our kitchenette.   It is the thought that counts.

My mother poured us each a glass of fresh milk from a small cream colored, floral patterned small mouthed pitcher.

As the glasses were filled one by one, I reflected on the sequence of steps that had brought this lactic beverage to the evening's meal.

"Can you bring in one of the cows for milking?" I had been asked a few hours earlier.

My mind had replied, "Who, me?", but my lips and tongue vocalized the response as "Sure."

It was a great honor, which is shorthand for a chore that entails responsibility, one that generated a shiver despite the heat of the midday July sun.

There was no need to ask which cow as it had been identified to me early in the morning when we kids had accompanied my uncle on his morning activities.

We were as much as an entourage as a nuisance for him, although to this day I am not certain where on the balance between pro and con he placed our annual two-week presence. Somewhere between a vacation and a fortnight of fever is the nearest scale that I can propose.

Back to our chosen milk giver. She, of course, we had learned that obvious distinction years previously, was black and white, and she ported real horns, an accessory that seemed to be fading rapidly from bovine fashion. Around her neck was a large, worn, brown strap, from which dangled a tarnished brass bell. Evidently, neither originated from the shelves of Tiffany's, but they served the dual purpose of positively identifying her as well as finding her easily, given the large size of the farm, whose cattle domain was comprised of open pasture in addition to many acres of woods, ideal shade during the summer months.

An hour later, I found myself alone on my mission. Quests are solitary ventures, but to be honest I was more concerned with survival than glory. I missed the comfort of my siblings, yet I concluded that if one of them had been selected instead of me, then I too would have remained absent. Although we teased each other about having been adopted, our shared sense of self preservation demonstrated our common gene pool.

As I regarded the cow, for she had no name, a few insects, also nameless, buzzed past my head, intent on important events in their brief lives. Would mine run longer? I smelled numerous anonymous flower fragrances that combined to offer without charge the aroma of High Summer.

Would this be the sole bouquet of my impending doom? My imagination was racing at full speed, aware of its own possible demise and endeavoring to complete its own outlandish bucket list.

If this simple chore went wrong, I would be gored, and stomped, becoming part of the countryside in a way heretofore inconceivable.

I shivered again, and for a reason unknown this motion reminiscent of winter brought to my mind the song The Twelve Days of Christmas and its maid a milking.

I was a boy of nine and if a five-year-old maid girl could milk a cow, then a boy of nine could fetch said cow. Only the following Noël did I learn the correct lyrics when I performed for the first time in a school play.

Although I remained frightened of the beast, and I assumed that it's up to now docility was a clever subterfuge, I was more afraid of failing my uncle than becoming part of his pasture.

Besides, I said to myself, I'm not defenseless.

I regarded the stick that I held in my bony hand, a tool that I had selected myself from the numerous that stood ready in the shop adjacent to the house. I had chosen the one that had struck my untrained eye as being the most capable, experienced, and proven.

My yet unstressed imagination had said derisively, "it's a bunch of sticks, pick one and let's go." Sometimes even those tasked with imagination have no creativity.

This was not just a stick, but a cattle stick. There is power in words, more so in precise words.

In the pasture, I looked at the cow and then again at my cattle stick.

It was about four feet long, as thick as my uncle's thumb, and it had the dark hue of a seasoned and polished branch of walnut.

"It is not walnut, it's birch," my mind corrected me, then it continued "the color comes from dried blood, probably from one of you cousins that they never talk about anymore."

I wanted so to switch off this annoying part of me. That was impossible, ignoring him as much as possible was the best that I could manage

I say cow but she had friends, dozens in fact. I had located her readily enough at her favorite watering hole, which in this instance was an actual watering hole, a farm pond.

It sat at the base of three intersecting slopes and was replenished by a small stream.

It may be that courage and wisdom are found at opposite ends of life's see-saw, yet I doubt that many of us would be thrilled by or contented with a permanent seat in its pivot zone

After coaxing, cajoling, and bizarre gestures on my part, targeted first at myself as a form of rehearsal, then directed at the cow, accompanied by bugling on her part, I was able to convince her to move.

Ten years later I would practice similar movements before dates.

Today I have no doubt that the cow was toying with me, enjoying her chance to perform before her troop with me, the debutant cowherd.

Tiring of a scene singularly lacking in memorable dialogue, being nine I had neither sophisticated language nor curses at my disposal, the cow began to move. Once she started all that remained for me to do was to congratulate myself while silently rendering thanks, and then to follow her.

It was a ten or fifteen minute hike back to the barn, following the well worn cow path across the pasture, through a wooded section where the hooves of countless passing had exposed the roots of several large hemlock trees.

The path was so deep and smooth that it's route through the grass on either side of it could have been followed readily in the dark.

Behind me I heard more cow bells as the entire herd was following. There were brown cows, and brown and white cows, and others with the same color pattern as mine, who I had now named Angie, at least for this trip. Angie was a sort of reddish bovine; it looked good on her. A bull followed along, but for my peace of mind I pretended that he had chosen to remain behind. Half grown calves were more difficult to ignore as they skittered in and out of procession and generally behaved as I supposed I did in similar human proceedings.

We finally entered the barn through its huge open door. I managed to guide only Angie to an open stanchion and closed it around her neck. She gave a toss of her head, causing the bell to clang as a sort of starting signal before she lowered her head to begin eating the treat of oats and buckwheat that lay before her.

Inside, the barn offered its own pleasant scent, one of fresh hay and clean straw and sleeping oats all mingled with that of free-range cattle, the sort of place a family of three could call home for a week in December.

Alfred was there, with a small, short, three-legged wooden milking stool. The sound of jetting milk squirting into a galvanized pail was evidence that the milking had commenced.

During the process, I was watched Angie from a foot away. Her large eyes and broad forehead were attractive, any sign of malevolence that I had only imagined was gone.

The milking was soon complete, the galvanized bucket that I mistakenly equated with terms such as pasteurized and homogenized now full.

Alfred carried the milk to the house where he would quickly strained it in a cursory manner, using relatively clean cheesecloth, into a floral pitcher saving the cream for the butter making that we kids would attempt the following day. He then set the porcelain vessel in the refrigerator

While my uncle performed this task, I released Angie from the stanchion, and she made her way back to her companions.

My mother finished pouring the milk, and while the large, thick specks of pale-yellow cream were not to my liking, and in fact repulsed my stay behind siblings, I made sure to drink every drop of Angie's gift and to confidently request another when I had finished the first glass of milk."

"Are you still awake, Linda?"

She smiled as way of answer.

"What is the moral of the story?"

"Does it need one? Did it entertain you?"

"Look around, Zeke. You have no competition when it comes to entertainment."

"Did you picture yourself back there in my past?"

"Very much so."

"Well, that event used to be in my future. Until it happened. The very best of the past used to not exist. You have to go through the future to get the past."

"So that's the moral?"

"Maybe. It could also be that it is healthy and polite to drink your milk, someone has gone to a lot of trouble to pour it for you."

"All that now to cry over spilt milk? Really Zeke Parks I expected more from you."

"People expect too much from attorneys, even retired ones. Its my turn to listen to your story."

"I met a man."

Zeke snorted water from his nose.

"Maybe I should stop now. I can't imagine that more words will generate a bigger reaction."

"You might be as surprised as I just was."

"He was the perfect one-night stand man."

"You are on a roll Linda," Zeke exclaimed before adding, "so to speak."

"Meeting him was why I moved to Brentville, one reason at least."

Linda paused to sip from her water bottle, prompting Zeke to ask innocently, "You aren't talking about Yellowstone, are you?"

As Linda choked at coughed at the unexpected query, Zeke said,

"We're even I guess."

"No, not Jerry,'" Linda said after she regained her breath.

"This man, I never learned his name. I never saw him but the once. And he is not why I stayed."

"Do you know how it is that you meet someone, maybe just once, like this man, maybe for a few brief moments, and you discover that your life will never be the same afterward?"

"I'm beginning to."

"He was in town for a funeral and," Linda paused, editing herself.

"And I was in town as well, staying for a few nights at the Barnier bed and breakfast. We struck up a conversation as people do."

"Have you read Heart of Darkness?"

"I saw the movie."

"It was like that, a story told in third or fourth-hand. I've even assigned the experience I had with him a title."

"Wow. That's novel. Your story already beats mine. What do you call it?"

"Shed of the Known."

"We were both staying at the Barnier house. I saw him several times as we entered or left our respective rooms, but up until our one conversation, we never exchanged more than a few pleasantries.

We were both outside on the wraparound porch, headed toward the swing. That isn't something that one does though, is it? To sit on a swing with a stranger?"

"It's legal in Brentville. Up to 10:30 on weekdays, 11 PM on Saturdays."

Linda laughed.

"I'm afraid that we violated a city ordinance then."

Linda ran her fingers through her hair as if to extract the memory in all its essence.

"We got to talking about the town, the number of churches. Upon arriving in Brentville, he had stared at the town's numerous churches, impressive in their quantity and beautiful to see.

The sheer number and evident craftsmanship frightened him. Could they, or one of them, be correct in the fervently held theory?

If their Heaven existed, that would be bad. Surely any afterlife would be unbearable in repetitiveness.

I mentioned that I could sit here over and over, quietly watching traffic not roll by, listening to the squeak of the overhead springs and under porch crickets.

'Things worth doing merit repetition.'

'I disagree. Nothing should be repeated or repeatable in the brief interval of this existence. As much as I can, I relive nothing, I simply live.'

'Like a...'

'An animal you want to say.'

'Do you dream? I mean do you have the same dreams over and over.'

'Who controls their dreams?'

'You don't repeat the everyday actions that I, that all of us do?'

'I brush my teeth every day, I eat most days, those are necessary. I breathe.'

"His tale was compelling. I admired his actions, but they filled me with dread. His chosen path terrified me. He recounted his life as a magnificent journey, but he was describing skydiving into the ocean to a woman panicked at heights and open water.

He talked of a fate that was horrible beyond imagination. That was his daily life. To live each day anew, can you picture an existence more awful?"

'You retained no stored photos of your childhood, or of your favorite people or places?'

'No, paper has weight, it becomes a burden more rapidly than I once thought. Linda, let me ask you, why are people enraptured by repetition?   Isn't it monotonous that each day is much of a muchness? Why add additional blandness. Life.is a boring school mistress who declines to vary her regimen, recess finds people playing the same identical game as they did yesterday and the day before. It is...'

'Comforting.'

'Smothering. Comfort is reserved for the ill and the weak. Life is hard.

It should be exciting, painful, full of the unexpected, and shed of the known.

The mundane must be abandoned. If you cannot shed yourself of these weights, then you should consign it to a box, a physical shed if you will, and burn it to the ground. This is not advice Linda, its simply my way.'

"He was gone the next morning. We never saw each other again. Undoubtedly, he does not regret it. I do."

"Why, Linda?"

"He embodied the future, he was in a strange sense my own personal devil, as realistic as anyone's. Is there a moral? Maybe, I don't know. The future is scary, it is better to not venture there."

CHAPTER TWENTY-SEVEN

It was the moment for any real gods to make an appearance.

She was pitied by others, diagnosed with a German sounding disease by highly educated and supremely confident practitioners of scientifically sponsored guessing. It would have made an excellent prime time game show, one that could in turn be sponsored by pharmaceutical companies proselytizing for their new cures, all of whose names sounded like minor, obscure and long forgotten Greek deities.

"Little do they know," the patient said to herself, a chuckle escaping from her throat. The unexpected sound was interpreted by all the medical staff there as confirmation of their collective judgment. The group's satisfaction was tinged with annoyance that a patient had the arrogance to laugh in their presence.

But she was senile, they murmured to each other to assuage their injured sensibilities.
She was senile, demented, another countless victim of Alzheimer's. It was a trinity of precise misses.
She chuckled again, more of a true laugh, the conscientious nurse noted on her electronic tablet, the flickering screen a stand-in for the patient's life chart.

In her bed, Gertrude pushed another persistent but tedious vignette from her mind, she had learned the value in abandoning the past.

She had long since passed the point in life where she was no longer expected to ask questions, followed soon thereafter by then milestone of not being permitted to pose questions. And then, weeks ago, clear signage that she was beyond deserving of answers. The exit was in sight. Passing away quietly only appears peaceful from the outside.

The past was an anchor on life's skiff and served only to delay the pleasures waiting around the next bend. Life leaned into the future like a skilled tango dancer. Leaning required a partner, a counterbalance and he was now absent. The strong man with thin lips and a powerful jaw was no longer able to prevent her lean from becoming a fall. She understood herself to be falling, but that was preferable to remaining in place. What was a fall, if not an exaggerated lean, the most daring of leans? Maybe he would reappear at the final moment to catch her. She had no faith in miracles but believed firmly in the power of her own imagination. She had always made her own world, we all do she had once concluded, but most people were hesitant to build one. They were afraid to lean.

Gertrude would, could lean into the future. She would will herself into the yet time, into the life to come, or not. It would be or it might not be, but it would not be the past.

The soulless equipment registered the termination of her vital signs. It did not note any last words, for that was not its metier.

They called it at the top of the hour. The staff breathed a collective sigh, unanimously pleased in their scientific precision, but the memory of her inexplicable laughter continued to reverberate in their minds.

CHAPTER TWENTY-EIGHT

"Come with me on a drive tomorrow. I promise not to do anything crazy like propose marriage."

"Maybe."

"Maybe what?"

"It depends on where we are going. It's not Rose Hill? Because if it..."

Zeke interrupted.

"No, it's not Rose Hill. We can save that for another time. Unless you have an unquenchable desire to see oddity perfected, I was going to propose, sorry it was a poor choice of words, to suggest a site, beautiful, peaceful, and quiet."

"I've been to the cemetery."

"No, its not the cemetery either."

"What's the special occasion?"

"Every occasion is special," Zeke replied with a wink.

"Its not the cemetery and it is not Rose Hill. Both are too near Brentville."

"Too near?"

"If you agree to leave Brentville purely for the day and alas not overnight Cinderella, it must be far enough away to qualify for the official Parks' day trip itinerary rules. I'm serious, although the exact rules are a work in progress."

Linda felt herself suddenly pulled away, as if the electricity had been cut, plunging her instantaneously into total darkness. But the sun was still shining. She was both there with Zeke and elsewhere, as if two days had collided. Time slowed to half speed, but the day shone with doubled brilliance. She found herself in this jumbled reality as a solitary bird watcher and simultaneously as a raptor.

She was soaring higher, drifting further away at the same time, the warm breath of the sun lifting her, soft air currents carrying her from one temporary home to another.

She was the watcher, focused on the black spot that grew smaller and then faded from sight.

It was nothing and everything.

"So, do we have an agreement?"

Linda blinked, her throat was dry, and her brain refused to command her head to raise to see the sky.

"To land somewhere," Linda whispered.

"It's a surprise."

"An arrival, a touch down in a wonderful land, invisible by those left behind, unseen from where I now."

"You can tell me afterward how you liked it."

"Could she really leave this town, even for a few hours," she wondered. The world that she had fled. The world was still spinning, possibly wobblier than ever with the eight billion humans waddling across it.

She had been an ant, scurrying across the shifting surface of the earth to avoid rising waters.

Mobs were breaking the society that she had known her entire life. The world as she understood it was fracturing, as if city streets had morphed into frozen ponds, the ice now cracking under her feet, snapping under the weight of every vehicle in America. She had sold her car, rented a house surrounded by natural grass, and had kept to sidewalks and footpaths. She was more than below the radar, she was counted by many as dead.

She believed that she had outrun the headlights of her future. She was safe in the past. Sick but safe.

Surrender might be a relief. It would be easy to join a mob. They were still in style, available anywhere, although she had not exactly seen any in Brentville.

"Don't make plans," Linda told herself."

"Zeke," she thought.

"Live as if each moment will last forever."

"Linda?" Zeke asked.

"Yes Zeke. Tomorrow is fine."

CHAPTER TWENTY-NINE

When she awoke, Linda imagined herself as an adult in her childhood home. But that was gone long ago, razed in fact if not in her memory. But she was more of a child in a newly rented home, comfortable in a rented bed, in today's Brentville, which itself did not feel rented at all.

Today was the day after Christmas morning, when the thrill of newly acquired toys was still fresh and sweet, more delicious in that there was no need to hurry downstairs to open them. The overwhelming sense of contentment brought a smile to Linda's lips.

"You're just another adult longing for childhood," Linda scolded herself.
"We mis-remember the past as drastically as we miscalculate the future. Can I be any more certain of the here?"

Before Brentville, she had visited her own village of origin, an urban village that may have once resembled Brentville in certain aspects, but which had now vanished. It was now deserted if not completely abandoned, a walk through its tree named streets, and alleys of yellow brick, exposed only decay. A once thriving village complete and vibrant, the plethora of businesses all either shuttered or demolished.

It was not even a shadow of itself. The yellow brick alley that had once led to play, to school, and eventually far away for herself, was still in places, overgrown here and there with weeds. The chicken coop owned by an elderly Polish couple was gone, as was the couple. The shoemakers, hardware stool, butchers, all erased to the point that even old photographs of them had likely been relegated to the rubbish. Public buildings like the post office and police station had been left to decay and eventual demolition. It was like attending a 50th high school reunion and wondering who had invited all of the old people. A few churches remained, silent testimony to the care of the faithful builders.

Were that it had been abandoned en masse, on schedule and then obliterated. It would have been kinder to the memories of the once former children of the town. Better to be blown up than it is to rust. Not the quote, but the same sentiment.

All the props of real life, hotels, bars, restaurants, doctors, dentists, bookstores, barbers, pharmacy, shops of all sorts, the list goes on. Gone in the blink of an eye that constitutes a century.

When a town center contains no public bench then it is a business, not a neighborhood.

Why had she returned? The desolation was expected, but vestiges of its former glory only emphasized the depth of the decay. The village contained no cemetery, for land was too precious to the living, but had now become nothing but a 150 acre monument to death.

Life is a transatlantic flight, the doors are closed, day becomes night, and then you arrive in daylight again, if lucky. And then the voyage commences again with a new load of passengers.

But she was safe in Brentville, her voyage nearly complete.

There was a financial firestorm burning, or exploding, or it lay just over the horizon. It was amazing, she had told herself, the entire country was in denial about the coming catastrophe. She had done her analysis, and bad times lay ahead. She had sold the market, not at its peak, but at a good price. She had acquired, with a portion of the proceeds, a nest full of tiny gold eagles.

Her own birds. They were not able to sing, but they could speak and were beautiful to behold.

180

She was comfortable here in this small town, off the proverbial beaten path. She would suffer, but not as much as most would, she would die, but not today. She would die, but in her own rented bed. She would watch the descent and the inevitable crash. It was even money as to whether she or the country would flounder first. It matttered little, the luxury of indifference would guide her through either calamity. She would endure for however long illness permitted. She had her flock of eaglets to protect her.

Without responsibility, time had slowed. At times, she wanted nothing as so much as sleep, but the summer sun called her early each morning and it was reluctant to release Linda, even as he waved goodbye each evening, disappearing below the skyline of the large Allegheny plateau.

The simple rise and set outshone any Youtube video. She refused to permit dreams that weren't hers anymore, particularly the ravings of marketing ghouls who desired her eyeballs.

"More cannibals," Linda said aloud.

"They are worse than any oversexed, single-minded man that I've batted away. They are worse than doctors, they do their utmost to have me purchase their imaginative but worthless products."

She drew a deep breath, reminding herself that it was time to rise

"Every breath that I take is eighty percent inert gas, the internet has succeeded in surpassing that level of nonvalue."

She looked at the smartphone that sat across the room, powered off until the upcoming Wednesday.

She smiled again, more broadly this time. The image of Hannah sprang into her mind. They were so similar, but they were on separate flights.

The young have as much in common with the elderly as the butterfly does to the caterpillar, the roles are simply reversed.

Hannah's future. With Linda's help it could be better, maybe even great, she mused.

Linda's newly limited exposure to the outside world confirmed her decision to withdraw to this sanctuary. The world was a jellyfish and Hanah deserved better.

"Humans were beasts, and it wasn't surprising that we murder each other but that we do it with such low frequency," she thought.

Linda was no longer smiling.

"Why do they call it the blues?" she asked herself.

"Blue is the most joyful color."

All these thoughts passed through her mind in the time it took the second hand to complete one circuit on the rented clock sitting patiently on the rented bedroom endtable.

She was safe in Brentville.

CHAPTER THIRTY

A mile from where Linda relished a few final moments of sleep, Hannah was awake.

Hannah ignored the absence of physical pain, taking for granted the health of youth as she sprang from the narrow bed.

Another day wasted she frowned. A calendar filled with clones of yesterday awaited her. Unless she acted. Today. Today was the day. It was a lie that she had grown tired of telling herself. It was now weeks of the same broken promise. Definitely today, she exclaimed vehemently.

But she had expressed the identical commitment with the same resolve yesterday.

"You will quit before the first frost," an inner voice jeered. "Emily has the right idea. You can find a decent man. One of those anglers. You could hook one of those," the voice continued, pleased with its cleverness.

"No catch and release necessary. Think about it Hannah, a year from now you could be delivering your own little minnow. Just in time for your first reunion. Married to a rich man, a mother, you would be queen of Brentville High."

For a second, Hannah believed in the devil, if not in good and evil, then a transitory faith in temptation. The devil must have so enjoyed high school, she thought, before banishing the annoying demon to non-existence.

But she believed in nothing apart from herself. School excelled at disinfecting students of all faith. Little was taught, and none encouraged. She had filled the vacuum with her own recital of worth.

The smart young believe in themselves.

Most others believe in everything else, for no matter how hard you scrub, morality doesn't wash off. It was a permanent stain.

A few believe in nothing at all.

Hannah had wondered what her contemporaries had done, but she had not dwelled upon it. Theirs were as valueless to her as she supposed hers to be in their eyes.

So many people, mobs and mobs of them. There were so many mobs today, maybe all the best spots were taken. But there was money in it if one got in on the ground floor, she had read about one mob whose founders were buying homes in all the best places, where one rubbed elbow with people from the best mob of all, the rich.

The dilemma remained. With evil gone, money must be the root of all happiness. What was it that Emily had mentioned. It would come to her. While she awaited its arrival, she thought about Emily.

She was perfect for Brentville.

"I should refer her to my departed demon," Hannah said aloud, qualmless about speaking to herself in either private or public.

"Do you pay finder fees?" she giggled to the absent minion.

"Emily and one of the fishermen. That would be great, a great capitalized and underlined. They could spawn where the fish weren't, and fish where the fish were. It would be perfect. More than that, it would be great."

Hannah stopped abruptly, remembering suddenly the words of Emily, about what she had seen in Linda's kitchen.

No, it was too dangerous, she thought of the boy, he'd likely end up dead or kill somebody in an attempt to impress her. She had to think longer, just a little longer, before acting.

Hannah would do as the detectors did, she would leave the paper and take the gold, only the gold. There was no need to think, as Linda preached, not when there was gold to be stuffed into her pockets.

"Linda is great, not Emily. Linda has exactly what I need. Today."

All was asquiet in the room as it had been a minute previously. But the old Hannah was gone forever, replaced by what? Hannah wondered, but only for a second, for she was now truly an adult.

She would be different, maybe not better, that did not matter to her, or anyone else. Better was passé, worthless. The internet had taught her well; only she mattered.

What was that old song that one of her so-called teachers liked. If it makes you happy it can't be all bad.

The boy had attempted to convince Hannah to join him, but she intuitively recognized him as an also ran, he would do her more harm than good, he would teach her nothing and she would pay a high price for it. No, if he were her only choice, then college and its debt were preferable.

The boy had nothing of value to offer Hannah. Moreover, he possessed nothing of value that she could tear from his hands. She questioned whether the grandfather's wealth was accessible. The boy had the fancy car, but she needed something plain, nondescript.

But now she had Linda.

"Linda is great."

Linda took an extra long shower, the clear water sparkling with the reflected gold and violet of the bathroom walls. The calming effect of the water and light was not working today. She felt nauseous, not sick, but worried.

She recognized this feeling that she was positive had faded long ago into nothingness. Love and panic were the same emotion.

She would expose herself to any drug, any false word. It was possible to believe anything for a while. And forever? That was a moment to grasp until the next forever offered itself.

And Zeke, was he a rung or the landing? She could not answer the question.

There are no answers in this uncertain world, no solutions, only handles to latch onto, progress defined solely by the imagined feel of her closed hand on another bar, possibly leading somewhere. It was enough. This was simply another day, the upcoming field trip with Zeke notwithstanding. There was no need to let loose of today's forever.

The small, beautiful church sat at a tiny crossroads. It was of dark carved stone. Inside, imported Italian tile flooring complemented the rose window fabricated from imported English glass.

As they circled the temple on foot, a strange sound came from the tall grass in the back, beyond the small graveyard that nestled next to the petite cathedral.

"What was that? Do you have a gun?" Linda asked excitedly.

"That was the sound of deer snorting. They don't enjoy being disturbed at lunch. And yes, I own a gun."

"Sorry."

Zeke laughed.

"This is the land of Bibles and guns. They play music in the sheriff's office where I pick up my concealed weapon permit. Its normal. If it came down to a choice, I'd choose the latter and I'd be in good company. Who would buy a used Bible? I mean, c'mon, who reads anymore? You can sell a used gun easily."

"I was afraid it was a bear."

"They are around, but they're shy. We also have Sasquatch and lost gold."

"UFOs?" Linda teased.

"We are working on it. They are so popular now though, even the government is getting into the game. Have you seen their latest claims?

Their involvement cuts into everyone's profits, and the fun of it. Do you see what I mean?

Oh, and what else? There are ghosts but then there are always ghosts, they are unreliable actors, but they work for nothing. Strange, isn't it?"

This new way of talking that Zeke had adopted, demanding agreement for each of his statements was aggravating. He must have something else on his mind. She felt already a soreness in her neck from this unaccustomed nodding.

Whatever was worrying him, she wished that he would get to it soon.

Zeke finished speaking, and Linda again signaled her approval with expected gesture, despite not having heard what he had said.

"I'd hoped that you would disagree," Zeke said, disappointed.

Linda froze.

"I must have misheard what you said."

"What do you think I said?"

"It doesn't matter. What did you say?"

"That you should move here."

"Why would I do that?"

"Then you aren't in favor of a move?"

"To here?"

It was Zeke's turn to nod yes.

"But there is nothing here Zeke."

Linda looked around.

"It's picturesque, but it needs more picture and less esque."

Zeke's head bobbed again.

"Exactly my feelings."

To the east was a ridge, covered in tall, majestic trees, while nearer, and to the south, were shorter monuments of granite.

"Do you think any of those large trees might have been carved with the initials of any of these people?" Zeke asked quietly.

Linda considered the question for a moment as the surroundings demanded seriousness.

"I hope so," was Linda's similarly muted response.

"Is it still enough for you?"

"Yes, it's very still. Serene. I'm not sure that I'd want to stop by in mid-winter."

"I agree. But you didn't answer my question."

"I didn't?"

"Is it still enough for you?" Zeke repeated the question, the time emphasizing the word still.

"Is Brentville sufficient for you? Does it satisfy your need?" he asked then paused before adding, "your need for nothingness?"

Linda said nothing.

"Look around Linda, this is the essence of what you seem to want, someone else's past, stripped of any quaintness. I thought that you might like to see what you're missing by living in Brentville. It's a halfway house. Not to me it isn't but that it how I see it when I try to peer through your eyes. Sometimes I don't need to imagine it. I look in your eyes and what I see reflected is not life."

Linda nodded and said, "I see". But she didn't. Nor did her nod signal approval. Nor did she particularly care to hear what he had to say. She understood only that it was important to him for him to tell her, to show her this place.

As if he had read her thoughts, Zeke spoke again.

"I thought it important to show you this nonplace, filled with nothing and nonpeople. Its only ten miles from New York State."

Zeke said New York as one word, like elbow.

"You could break your lease and relocate here, if you find it as irresistible as I don't."

"You really know how to impress a girl, Zeke Parks," Linda joked, then added somberly, "Thank you."

They left the pretty roadside church, Linda thinking that the small centuries old building was still able to perform miracles. She felt better on the return trip than she had in many months.

They passed by oddly named villages, Ulysses, and Gold, and Roulette. Along the way they stopped in the village of Kersey for gasoline and ice cream, where Linda surprised Zeke by ordering a triple scoop, which she explained away by claiming, "A girl deserves a consolation prize Zeke, after such a shocking non-proposal."

188

Nearing Brentville, a crow lifted from the offside shoulder, its beak closed around an appetizer sized morsel of fresh roadkill. Zeke tapped the brakes momentarily, slowing the vehicle's speed just enough to grant the bird sufficient time to traverse the country road, a meter above the road's surface.

"Do you see that Culligan building?" Zeke asked.

"Yes."

"Years and years ago, it used to be on the south side of town, near where the hospital is. It was the perfect landmark to use when giving directions. After the move, it was confusing, the directions were instantly inaccurate. But nothing else had changed.

You know Linda, its ok to change your mind," Zeke said softly as they pulled onto Snowden.

"It doesn't change who you are."

"I enjoyed today, Zeke."

"Me too, Linda. Maybe another day trip soon?"

"Yes, that would be fun."

Linda's mind stalled when she saw the Odyssey in her driveway. Had it returned like a lost pet. It made no sense.

"Whose van is that?" Zeke asked, and was just as perplexed as Linda, when she replied.

"It used to be mine."

She and Zeke stepped through the unlocked door of the house.

The body was still warm. Hannah lay on the stairs, her left cheek on the floor, and her body extending up four or five steps. Gold coins were scattered halfway up the staircase, with a few encircling Hannah's head like a halo. A gold necklace encircled her neck, its Australian kangaroo gold piece rested on the hardwood floor like a grudgingly earned medal. Small clumps of potting soil were visible on several of the steps, and Hannah's hands were streaked with the same black-brown earth.

A metal detector lay in the upper third of the long staircase, buzzing excitedly. Otherwise, the house was silent, as if the scene was new age performance art, the artist expectant of applause. But it was death draped in its ancient fashion of finality.

189

It was only when Linda noticed that Hannah was wearing jeans that she screamed, screams that were echoed eventually by those of a police car.

The official report determined that Hannah had been tripped by the metal detector when she was scurrying down the twenty-four step staircase on her second break-in. The gold stolen on the first attempt was never recovered, thereby dividing locals into two camps, one who believed that Linda Smith was attempting a big city girl insurance fraud, and the other camp, which proceeded to acquire every metal detector in the county.

CHAPTER THIRTY-ONE

The girl's future was now confined those townsfolk with whom she had wanted nothing so much as to abandon to their past.

Linda often wished it were her rather than the girl. Linda had moved to Brentville to reclaim a past that, if it had ever existed outside of her imagination, was no longer to be found in this town. Her attempt at construction had failed, she should have left undisturbed the historical district. In lieu of building a past, she had destroyed two futures.

If Eden was populated with flora and fauna before the first couple, then why did they too have to leave? An entire planet banished due to actions of two ignoramuses who by the prosecutor's own claim, were incapable of distinguishing right from wrong.

"But you and I, Hannah, we knew the difference, and this time only those who are guilty are forced out. I guess that is a better justice. I understand how brief my remaining time is. It's more reason to leave."

Brentville, or her dream of it, had proven to be a delusion, nothing more than a temporary respite from the pain of real life. Had it been a self prescribed chemotherapy, one without nausea but seemingly just as ineffective?

Every choice she had made in life seemed to have been wrong. She had built a stage of her own desire, written the script, but it had been twisted against her will into a tragedy that would play better in the town's opera house than it had here in her private rented theatre.

Linda deposited her sparse belongings into the trunk of the car that she had had to buy. She had hoped to never own another automobile. She had hoped a lot of things.

Linda was unable to do a final walkthrough. The gay yellow of the bathroom sickened her. It seemed that the walls were stuccoed with vomit. If she had forgotten anything, so be it. It was time to forget.

The past months had been a fantasy, a dream that she had insanely attempted to carve into the waters of North Fork. It was now her time to flow, to leave this village, worse than she had found it, like a deadly flood that lived on in the town's memory.

She could not say goodbye. She would flee, as she had before, so long ago it seemed. As Mike Hayes had fled. She could not say goodbye to the house, to the neighbors, not to Zeke, not to Mike.

Perhaps this was all a dream, and there is no sense in bidding farewell to dreams.

The girl was now forever on the future side of the town's life, carried there in a hearse that was a dark twin to the car that she had stolen.

Linda too must rejoin the future, a future anywhere but here.

In the beginning she had envisioned the town leaving its imprint on her. At a minimum, she had expected to find peace within its small, invisible borders.

Instead, Linda had scarred her adopted parent, not deliberately, and not permanently, she prayed to all the gods whose homes she had visited.

Ancient trees, timeless rocks, cathedrals, and churches all were sent the same impassioned plea.

The girl would rest in Linda's assigned spot, the one Linda had bought after signing the lease on the house on Snowden.

She would not suggest that the town forgive her fatal act. That would be too cruel. This entire episode was proof of fate's brutality.

Nor would the town forget. She could hope that in some distant future the Historical Society or local theatre group could benefit from this tragedy that she had bequeathed them.

Absent Linda's arrival in Brentville, Hannah would be alive. If the girl had not been rushed by Linda's return, the gold and the car would have disappeared, with Hannah whisked into a future brighter than the none that covered her now.

The car had been insured by Cassie, and Linda had more gold.

Yes, both of us could be alive, should be alive, as alive and as content as any pair of random women can be.

She would leave the town money, alms for her and something, she was unable to describe it to herself, for the family. Restitution? An insult?

A fine? A combination of those and other ingredients more emotional; sorrow, regret. It would not be adequate, but it would have to do. Without intent, she had done her worst, this act was her deliberate best.

A true repair was beyond the grasp of any living being.

Linda had arrived in Brentville anticipating her death. She had failed in that too. The town had cured her, despite her terminal self diagnosis. Linda was healed and yet cursed, leaving Eden for what? A promised land. She did not deserve one but possibly Hannah did. On this planet of billions, surely someone did. So where was this promised land, this second or third or fourth choice?

They say that time heals all wounds. Its not true. It simply buries the wounded, sooner or later.

Linda settled herself behind the steering wheel and pulled onto the residential street. She drove on, her eyes locked straight ahead, not glancing at the buildings nor at the people that constituted what for a moment had been her home.

Linda refused to look in the rear-view mirror, the past was best ignored.

When she arrived at the intersection with the interstate highway, Linda paused. Her head swiveled slowly several times, left to right, left to right. There was no oncoming traffic in either direction. Left, or right? East? Or West?

Both led to the future.

Finally, Linda turned the steering wheel and pressed confidently on the accelerator.

EPILOGUE

Emily stood beside the two male diners seated in her section. Her habitual smile was unconscious, despite the loss of Hannah, and now the departure of Linda.

She had learned so much from the two women.

Now she was on her own, alone in Brentville. Friends, family, and townspeople assured her that she would be fine, time would pass. She had her entire future before her. Time moves on. All the appropriate murmurings were directed her way.

Across the restaurant, Mike Hayes and Uncle Zeke were discussing their new business venture, maps of the region and a copy of Stone Church in the Wood lay between them.

Out of the corner of her eye, Emily glimpsed a passing semi-tractor trailer. Like these two strangers sitting here, deciding what to order, the vehicle was another transient.

She had heard them discussing lost gold. Detectors. They would never stop arriving in Brentville. If anything, their numbers had increased. Whether it was the lure of Civil War treasure or the search for Hannah's horde, a term she had heard with increasing frequency, it mattered not at all to Emily, except in the sense that detectors tipped well, for, without exception, they believed in good luck.

Luck. As far as Emily knew, the word luck was mentioned in no scripture. Did its absence deem it a false god? Emily understood that there were so many false gods, she had learned that lesson well. In contrast there were but a few true ones.

Linda's stay in Emily's town had been brief yet impactful. But now, with Linda gone, what the locals had begun calling the old Smith house would likely have a new tenant, Emily told herself.

Soon, maybe in a few months, she would enjoy living there herself. Emily knew the house so well. She remembered Mrs. Dietz, the long-term owner whom Emily had visited as part of her meals on wheels, bicycle wheels in Emily's case. Mrs. Dietz had died last week in hospice; Emily's father had told her. The funeral had been sad, but not nearly as sad as Hannah's.

Hannah, gone. Her departure had been so sudden and unexpected. It was an immediate loss, as irretrievable as dropping the baton in a relay.

The memory of Hannah's last event, the final moments of Hannah's life, flashed through Emily's mind again: the accident with the metal detector, the tumble, the horrific crack as flesh and skull impacted hardwood floor.

It would have been immoral to have removed Hannah's share of gold from her dead body after that tragedy. Still, half of the metallic fortune was more than enough to provide a wonderful life for Emily. She had taken one final look at Hannah's corpse, and then exited out a side door, scurrying through the woods that led to the street below.

Perhaps it was a blessing in disguise. Hannah and Emily would have gone their own ways in any case, the friendship would only grow more distant and then disappear. That had been their plan and the unspoken outcome. Neither of them however, had expected the separation to be so abrupt and final.

Poor Hannah, all those months of pole vaulting without mishap and she died tumbling down a staircase. As near as Emily remembered it, for Emily had not measured the distance at the time, but she knew the house so well, didn't she, Hannah had dropped eleven feet to her death. It had been Hannah's new and final morbid personal best.

Emily's smile widened at her memory of the future to come. One day, locals would refer to the residence on Snowden Avenue as Emily's house, the name Smith forgotten.

Emily's smile flattened for a moment. She would decide later whether or not to redo the bathroom. The golden highlights were pretty, after their own fashion. Did she love it or not? It was an important question, but she had tomorrow and the day after to reflect on it.

Her sister Mary and Hunter had broken up. That outcome was obvious from the moment that Mary had begun discussing piercings and tattoos.

"Pierced belly buttons. It prepares one for pain," Hannah had warned Mary.

"Hunter is not like that," Emily repeated to herself silently.

"He's great," Emily said, the smile returning.

The two male diners smiled in return, misinterpreting Emily's intent.

She faced one of them and asked pleasantly, "Would you like a refill on your coffee, honey?"

www.ingramcontent.com/pod-product-compliance
Lightning Source LLC
Chambersburg PA
CBHW020325260626
47156CB00004B/1382